BOOK of legion

Blood & Grace

ja huss

BADLANDS MC
BOOK 2

BLOOD & grace

Book of Legion - Badlands MC #2
A Dark Outlaw Biker Serial Romance

New York Times Bestselling Author
JA HUSS

BLOOD AND GRACE
Copyright © 2026 by JA Huss
Cover design by JA Huss
Interior design by JA Huss
ISBN: 978-1-957277-61-5
All rights reserved.

No part of this book may be reproduced in any form or by any electronic or mechanical means, including information storage and retrieval systems, without written permission from the author, except for the use of brief quotations in a book review.

Outlaw Clubhouse.
Public Claiming.
Loyalty Test.
Church At Dawn.

Down on your knees—it's time to choose sides.

ABOUT THE BOOK

Forty-seven thousand acres of Ashby land. Six generations of Montana dynasty. And one daughter who was never going to be allowed to choose a man called Legion.

They were caught at the silo at midnight. Same place they've been hookin' up for years.

While Savannah's fiancé had her bound to a bed and drugged out of her mind, Legion was getting the life beat out of him by a bunch of cowboys.

Her family thought violence would be enough to end it.

They were wrong. It only made the bond stronger.

Now Savannah has to prove what it means to stand by her man and Legion has to convince forty-seven patched members of the Badlands MC that protecting her will be worth it.

Outlaw clubhouse.

Public claiming.

Loyalty test.

Church At Dawn.
BLOOD AND GRACE
Down on your knees—it's time to choose sides.

Inside the pages you can expect:
- 🏍️⛓️‍💥🔥 Outlaw Biker Romance
- 💸🖤🔧 Rich Girl / Poor Boy
- ⛓️‍💥🔒🖤 Property Of
- 🖤🫦🗡️ Morally Gray/Anti-Hero MMC
- 🔥👁️⛓️‍💥 Obsessed/Possessive MMC
- 🚫🖤🫦 Forbidden Love
- 👪🫂🖤 Only Her
- 🖤🗡️👪 Only Him
- 💚🏚️🌫️ Childhood Sweethearts
- 🗡️🔪💀 Touch Her and Die
- 🔥🍆🩸 Primal Spice
- 🫣🔐🖤 Secret Relationship

CHAPTER 1
SAVANNAH

I wake slowly to bright light and soft piano music. The kind of light one finds in hospitals and forces you to squint, the kind of music one finds in elevators that forces you to forget.

My head is throbbing and feels… too full. Like it's stuffed with cotton. The nasty taste in my mouth has me craving water. I try to move my hand to my face, but I can't.

I'm tied down.

The panic is immediate. My eyes fly open. The ceiling swims into focus—knotty pine beams. A chandelier made from antlers. Hunting cabin.

An Ashby hunting cabin.

I pull against whatever's holding my wrists.. Hard and unyielding. Not rope. Zip ties.

I can move my legs a little and I feel air on my thighs. I'm still wearing my dress, but it's hiked up and this is when I remember.

I'm not wearing underwear.

Legion.

The silo.

Oh God.

"Legion," I whisper, my voice cracking. The memory slams back—flashlights cutting through darkness. Cash's voice. Men dragging Legion away. His body hitting the ground. Blood.

"He can't hear you, darling." Marcus's voice makes my skin crawl. I turn my head and there he is, sitting in an armchair by the fireplace. Watching me. Smiling.

"Where is he?" My throat feels raw. From screaming. I was screaming for Legion.

"Don't worry about him." Marcus rises, straightens his slacks. Still dressed like we're at a country club. "Are you thirsty? You must be parched."

Wrong. This is wrong. All wrong.

"Untie me." I try to sound firm, but my voice trembles.

"In time." He moves to a small table, pours water into a glass. "You need to rest first. You've had quite the shock."

Shock?

I test the restraints again. Tight. Professional. "Marcus, this isn't funny. Untie me now."

He approaches with the glass, a bendy straw poking out the top. Like I'm in a hospital. Like he's helping.

"Careful now," he says, holding the straw to my lips. "Small sips."

I'm so thirsty I drink despite myself. The water tastes clean, at least.

"Where am I?" I ask, when he pulls the glass away.

"Somewhere safe." He smiles. That campaign smile.

Perfect teeth. Dead eyes. "The north ridge cabin. No one will bother us here."

North ridge. Miles from the main house. Miles from anyone.

"My brothers—"

"—know you're with me." He sets the glass down, then brushes hair from my forehead with cool fingers. I flinch. "Everyone's very concerned about your... episode."

"Episode?"

"Your breakdown, sweetheart. After what that criminal did to you."

The fire crackles as logs shift. I'm suddenly aware of framed photographs on the walls. My face. Over and over. Childhood shots. Riding competitions. One of us at a charity gala. All perfectly arranged.

Like a shrine.

"I didn't have a breakdown," I say carefully. "And Legion didn't do anything to me I didn't want."

Marcus's smile doesn't waver, but something flickers behind his eyes. "You're confused. That's understandable after trauma."

"I'm not confused, Marcus. I want you to untie me. Right now."

He ignores this, moving to retrieve a tray from the small kitchenette. "You should eat something. I made your favorite."

The tray holds a plate of food. Mashed potatoes. Roast chicken. Green beans. A meal I've never once told him I liked.

"Marcus, please." I soften my voice. Sunday manners. The ones Mama taught me for dealing with difficult men. "I'd feel much better if I could sit up properly."

"Soon." He sits on the edge of the bed. Too close. "First, let me take care of you."

He scoops up mashed potatoes with a silver spoon. Holds it to my lips.

"I can feed myself if you untie me."

"Open wide," he says, like I'm a child.

I press my lips together. His eyes harden.

"*Savannah*." The single word is a warning. "Don't be difficult."

My survival instinct kicks in. *Play along, Savannah. For now.*

I open my mouth. The potatoes are still hot. Not terrible. Butter and garlic. But my stomach turns as he watches me chew with naked satisfaction.

"Good girl," he murmurs, wiping a bit from the corner of my mouth with a cloth napkin. "See? I take good care of what's mine."

Mine.

I swallow hard. "Marcus, what happened to Legion?"

He feeds me another spoonful before answering. "That's not important."

"It is to me."

"He got what was coming to him." His voice remains pleasant. Conversational. "Men like that always do."

Fear claws up my throat. "Is he—"

"Let's not talk about him." Marcus cuts a piece of chicken. "Let's talk about us. Our future."

"There is no us." The words slip out before I can stop them.

His hand freezes midair. "Don't say that, darling. Not after everything I've done for you."

"What have you done, Marcus?" My voice sounds strange to my own ears. Distant. "Tied me to a bed? Drugged me?"

"Protected you." He sets the fork down, leans closer. "Saved you from yourself." His breath smells like mint and whiskey. His cologne—expensive, sandalwood—fills my nostrils.

"I don't need saving."

"Oh, but you do." He traces my jawline with one finger. "You always have. That's why your mother chose me."

"My mother is dead."

"But her wishes live on." His finger trails down my neck. "And I promised her I'd take care of her little girl."

My skin prickles up. "When did you ever speak to my mother?"

"We had an understanding." His smile turns secretive. "About what was best for you."

Lie. Has to be. Mama never even met him.

"Please." I try again, making my voice small. Helpless. The way men like him want women to sound. "I really need to use the bathroom."

"There's a catheter for that."

My blood turns to ice. "A what?"

"I thought of everything." He resumes feeding me, as if discussing the weather. "We might be here a while. Until you're better."

"Better from what?" Panic rising. Chest tight. And suddenly, that feeling like I need to pee, isn't the need to pee but… he put a fucking tube up inside me? What. The hell.

"Your confusion," Marcus says. He wipes my mouth again. "Your rebellion."

"Marcus, this is kidnapping."

He laughs, genuinely amused. "You can't kidnap your own fiancée, silly."

"I'm not your fiancée anymore." I look pointedly at my bare finger. "I left the ring at home."

His smile doesn't falter. "It's right here." He pats his pocket. "Ready when you are."

"And if I'm never ready?"

Something shifts in his eyes. Something cold and patient.

"Then we wait," he says simply. "I have all the time in the world."

Marcus circles the bed with the measured steps of a preacher delivering his most important sermon, each footfall echoing his righteous certainty. "You've been under his influence for years, Savannah. That kind of manipulation runs deep in the psyche. But we'll work through this together, step by step, until you're cleansed of it."

Together. Like we're equal partners in my salvation. Like these ropes binding me to this bed are just loving restraints for my own protection.

"He's dangerous," Marcus continues, voice dripping with feigned concern. "A criminal. The way we found you two, Savannah. Together." His lip curls with such disgust, it almost comes off rehearsed. "He was inside you. You had his come all over your legs. That's not love, darling. That's fucking. Possession. Predatory grooming."

Grooming. "What the hell are you talking about? He didn't groom me. We were childhood sweethearts."

Marcus makes a sad face at me. He's insane. "Your mother warned me about him extensively. Said he'd been fixated on you since childhood. Stalking you. Taking advantage of your innocent nature."

Well, that's definitely a lie. Eleanor Ashby loved Legion Kane. Maybe in ways I don't want to think about. She's got twenty or thirty thousand pictures of him to prove it.

Marcus has lost his mind.

"We'll get you the absolute best help, darling," he continues. "Intensive therapy. Specialized trauma counseling. Whatever resources you need to process and heal from the psychological damage Legion Kane inflicted on you."

He's the trauma. He's the one damaging me. I am kidnapped. Tied to a bed by my fiancé. *Former fiancé*, I correct myself.

Suddenly, his hand is on my thigh, proprietary and cold as marble. He slides it up under my dress hem with entitled certainty.

I go rigid, bile burning up my throat.

Oh, God.

Again, the realization that I have no underwear on hits me. I didn't wear any because... well, there's exactly one reason I meet Legion Kane at the Silo. And it's so he can claim me completely, desperately, anyway he wants. My eyes squeeze shut, heart racing as forbidden memories surface of his rough hands, his hungry mouth, his—

Marcus's fingers trace clinical patterns on my bare skin. Goosebumps rise in pure revulsion. I want to scream until my throat bleeds. To kick until bones break. To bite until I taste blood.

But I remain perfectly still. Motionless as a photograph in Eleanor's portfolio.

He's touching places Legion just—No. Lock that memory away. Don't let him taint it. Keep it sacred. Keep it yours alone.

"It's all right," Marcus says. "He defiled you, I totally understand your revulsion. But I took care of that."

"Took care of what?" I blurt. My heart is breaking. Have they killed Legion? "Where is Cash? Where are my brothers?"

"They helped me, Savannah."

"*Helped you do what?*"

"Clean you. Bring you up here so you could rest."

"Clean… *clean* me? What the hell does that mean?"

"I washed you, darling. I washed away all traces of him. Inside and out."

Oh, god. I actually turn my head to the side and almost puke. He was touching my body while I was unconscious. He *cleaned* me!

I've never felt so utterly exposed. So deeply violated. Never, in my entire life.

Marcus either doesn't notice my visceral reaction or simply doesn't care. He withdraws his hand and turns to study the photos he's meticulously arranged on every wall like some twisted gallery.

My entire life displayed like art.

Me at six, clutching a blue show ribbon with gap-toothed pride.

Me at twelve, weaving wildflowers into delicate crowns with sun-browned fingers.

Me at sixteen, caught in a rare moment of genuine laughter, bathed in golden prairie light.

He moves between them like a possessive curator, adjusting frames with precise fingers, wiping away invisible dust with reverent care.

What kind of sick set up is this? Why are all these pictures of me on the walls? They do not belong here. This is a hunting cabin. No one comes up here.

Which makes it the perfect place for a kidnapping.

He must be lying about Cash and Wyatt helping. He has to be. And there is no way—no fucking way in hell—that Colt would have anything to do with this.

Where is Colt?

Where is Legion?

I might never know the answers to these questions if I don't get out of here. Who can tell how crazy Marcus is right now? He put a fucking tube up inside me to collect my urine so he doesn't have to let me out of bed!

I pull against the restraints, testing. "I will never be with you again, Marcus."

His smile doesn't falter. Just shifts—a careful rearrangement, like adjusting a tie before stepping onto a stage. "You're confused, Savannah. That's perfectly natural after trauma."

"The only trauma here is being tied to a bed by you."

He leans forward, fingertips pressed together like a therapist I never asked for. "Your mother warned me this might happen. That if he ever got to you again—"

"My mother is dead."

"But her wisdom lives on." His voice softens to that political cadence he uses at fundraisers. "You're Savannah Ashby. Not some biker's plaything."

"I chose him."

"You chose escape. Rebellion. It's textbook, darling."

I stare at the ceiling. The knotty pine beams are unfinished. Rough. Like Legion's hands. "Untie me."

"When your mind is stable, my love. I'm going to help you recover. And then we can talk about letting you make your own decisions."

"Decisions like… when I'd like to go to the bathroom? Decisions like… holding a spoon to feed myself? I'm not an infant, Marcus. I'm not crazy."

"Of course not." He stands, smoothing invisible wrinkles from his slacks. "You're wounded. And I'm patient enough to wait."

"For what?"

"For you to remember who you really are."

"I know exactly who I am."

His laugh is gentle, practiced. "The woman I know wouldn't spread her legs against a silo wall for a convicted felon."

The words don't even register. He thinks this is embarrassing me? It's not. I have 'spread my legs' for Legion Kane hundreds of times. I'm ashamed of none of them.

"I'm going to bring you dessert later," Marcus says, like we're discussing normal plans. "Something sweet. Your body needs care after what it's been through."

"What have you done to Legion?"

He ignores me, straightening a photo frame. "Your

mother built something beautiful with you, Savannah. A legacy. I won't let him destroy that."

"What did you do to him?"

"What needed to be done." He walks to the door and opens it. "Rest now. We'll talk when you're more yourself."

He walks through and the lock clicks behind him.

Heavy. Deadbolt.

I wait thirty seconds, counting heartbeats, making sure he's gone. Then I pull hard against the restraints, methodical now. Testing their give.

Zip ties. Not rope. Wrapped around each wrist, secured to the headboard's wooden slats. My ankles too, spread just wide enough to make me feel vulnerable. Clinical. Like I'm prepped for examination.

The plastic bites when I twist my wrists, but there's a technique to breaking zip ties. I saw it once in a crime documentary. You raise your hands above your head, then bring them down hard against your chest, using the momentum to snap the plastic.

But my hands are secured separately. No momentum possible.

I need another way.

The cabin's familiar. I've been here for family hunting trips, summer escapes, winter holidays. No cell service. One bathroom. Two bedrooms. Kitchen. Living area.

And tools. Always tools in a hunting cabin.

I study the restraints again. The zip ties connect to rope, which threads through the headboard slats. Smart. Harder to break free this way.

I rotate my wrists slowly, feeling for weakness.

There isn't much, but the plastic will eventually fatigue if I work at it consistently. Plastic always does.

I close my eyes and listen. No sounds outside. No vehicles. No voices. Just wind in pine needles and distant water—the creek that runs behind the property.

Breathe. Think. Plan.

I start working my right wrist in slow, methodical circles. The plastic doesn't give—not yet—but it will.

It has to.

CHAPTER 2
LEGION

I come back in pieces. First, the pain—cataloged, filed away. Then sound—wind through wooden slats. Then awareness—my hands bound behind me, my shoulders wrenched backward against a support beam.

Rope, not cuffs.

Blood has dried tacky across my face. Left eye swollen to a slit. Two ribs are definitely cracked on my right side.

My breathing is shallow and uncontrolled. I feel like I can't get enough of it. Like I need to gulp it like water.

But I've been in worse situations. Not a good thing to admit to yourself when you're in the middle of being kidnapped and restrained by an Ashby militia of two, but it is what it is.

I keep my head slumped, chin to my chest, and try to control my breathing. There are two other people here. When I lift my eyes up, I see Wyatt at the window. He's looking out, fingers tapping against glass. Cash paces the room.

They smell like money, even from here.

I'm in what appears to be a hunting shack. Off grid if the one kerosene lamp burning somewhere to my right is anything to go by. It's still dark. Same night? If so, it's the wee hours of the morning.

But there's no telling how long I've been out. Could already be tomorrow for all I know.

I've been in this cabin before. Eleanor took pictures of me everywhere. And after I turned eighteen, these photo shoots got more and more… planned. Professional. If these fucking boys knew just how well I knew their mother, they'd kill me.

Bad enough I know their sister better.

Savannah.

Just thinking her name makes my heart hurt. Just picturing her, up against the silo wall, skin silver in the moonlight. Her mouth on mine, her body arching. Then light, sudden and brutal. Her brothers. Men with rifles.

Her scream as they dragged her away, still echoing in my skull.

The rage builds slow and cold. It doesn't cloud my thinking—it sharpens it. Makes everything crystalline.

If they've hurt her, I'll tear this place apart with my teeth. I'll hunt them across every acre of their precious ranch. I'll become the demon they named me.

Even if she's untouched, they're all dead men walkin' to me.

They just don't know it yet.

I keep my breathing steady, my body slack. Let them think I'm still unconscious while I allow my mind the freedom it craves to plan revenge.

Patience is just rage on a longer fuse.

Suddenly Cash mutters, "Family fucking legacy." His voice is pitched low but meant to be heard. "Six generations of Ashbys, and this is what it comes to." His boots stop. I can feel him lookin' at me. "Trailer trash with prison ink thinking he has rights to what's ours."

He starts moving again, faster now. Agitated.

"She was supposed to marry well. That was the deal. That was always the fucking deal." A thud as his fist hits something wooden. "Mother made it clear. The land passes through the bloodline. And what does Savannah do? Spreads her legs for a Kane."

He says my name like it's something rotten in his mouth.

Wyatt is still standing by the window, a darker shadow against the night. He doesn't speak, but his silence feels like judgment. The patient kind. The kind that waits for you to move wrong before it pulls the trigger.

I test the rope binding my wrists. Tight, but not professional. There's give where the fibers cross. If I work it right, I can make space. Just need time.

"Three fucking years we kept her clean," Cash continues, circling back to where he started. Like a dog chasing its tail. "Three years rebuilding what he destroyed. And the minute he's out—"

He kicks something that skitters across the floor. I keep my breathing even, head down. I'm counting steps to the door. Measuring the distance to Wyatt's boots. Calculating how much blood I can afford to lose and still make it to the tree line.

"Where the hell is Colt?" Cash suddenly demands,

voice dropping to a harsh whisper. "He was supposed to be here."

Wyatt clears his throat. "Said he couldn't make it."

"Couldn't *make it*?" Cash's voice rises. "This is family. This is Savannah."

"He's been... different lately." Wyatt's voice is measured, careful. "Past few months, he's barely at the ranch. Misses meetings. Doesn't answer calls."

"That's not like him."

"No," Wyatt agrees. "It's not."

A pause stretches between them, loaded with something I can't quite name.

I keep my face slack, storing this away. Something's off with the brother. Something they don't understand yet.

Cash's head snaps toward me, eyes narrowing like he's just realized the prey he thought was dead is still breathing.

"Well, look who decided to wake up." He crosses the room in three strides, crouches until his face is level with mine. His breath smells like whiskey and entitlement. "You think I don't see what this is? What you're doing?"

I stare back, let my silence fill the space between us.

"Savannah Ashby doesn't belong to you." He says her name like it's property with a deed attached. "She never did. She never will. That girl was born for something better than some ex-con's come stain on her family name."

The rope burns against my wrists as I work it, but my face stays still. Dead-eyed. Prison-calm.

"You think I don't know?" Cash's voice drops lower.

"You've been circling our family since you were a kid. My mother—" He stops, jaw working. "Eleanor saw something in you. God knows what. Took all those pictures."

My pulse quickens, but I don't give him the satisfaction of a reaction. Just keep breathing through the blood in my mouth.

The rope gives another quarter inch. I keep working.

"You think those pictures meant something, Kane?" Cash laughs, but it sounds hollow. "That you meant something to her? You were just another one of her projects. Like those fucking coffee table books. 'Montana Wildlife: Trailer Park Edition. That's all you were. Trailer blood doesn't get to rewrite legacy. Doesn't get to touch what's been Ashby since before Montana was a state." He's preaching now, to himself more than me. "You're just a footnote. A phase. The mistake Savannah needed to make before finding what's real."

I say nothing. Let my silence hum with defiance. With the knowledge that Savannah came to *me*. That she chose *me*.

Cash leans in closer, his voice dropping to a whisper like we're sharing a secret.

"She's with Marcus now," he says, each word measured, precise. "Where she belongs. With a man who can keep her name clean."

My jaw locks. Something hot and black swells behind my eyes.

"Had to drug her, you know. Just a little something to calm her down. You make her crazy." He tilts his head, studying me like I'm something under glass. "She was hysterical. Screaming. Scratching. Not herself."

I focus on the rope, on the slow give of fibers.

"Marcus had to wash her down." Cash's lips curl slightly. "Your filth was all over her thighs. Inside her. Had to clean that out, too."

The demon rises in me—not some fairy tale bullshit, but the thing I've carried since I was a boy. The thing that knows exactly how to break a man's neck with a quarter-turn more than necessary.

"She's sleeping now. When she wakes up, we're gonna cut the memory of Legion Kane out of her. She'll never think about you again. Won't ever miss fucking her trailer-boy in that silo. You think I didn't know, all growing up, that's where you two met? Shit... Eleanor had pictures of that too. Sick fuck, that's what you are. Did you tell my mother that you were fucking her daughter at the silo? Is that why she was there?" Cash's voice has the rhythm of scripture, like he's practiced these words.

Privately, I am a bit stunned at this news. I had no idea Eleanor ever took pictures of Savannah and me out at the silo. Never even suspected it.

Is Cash lying?

I stop listening. Just watch his mouth move.

He better be lying.

Because if Eleanor was taking pictures of Savannah and me... well... that paints a pretty sick picture in my mind. And to be honest, I was just barely coming to terms with the sickness I already knew about.

I don't need this too.

"You hear me, Kane?" Cash stands up and gives me a kick in the ribs. The pain is sharp and real.

Then, before I can catch my breath, he kicks me in

the chest too. A sharp, silver-tipped boot lands square inside my brand. The pain swells. Something worse than being burned alive. Broken ribs and rotting flesh.

Stars swim in the blackness behind my eyes.

"Badlands," Cash sneers. "There's not gonna be a rescue, Kane. It's over for you."

In my head, I'm already standing. Already moving. Already watching Wyatt's eyes go wide as I drive his own rifle stock through his sternum. Already feeling Cash's throat collapse under my thumbs.

I name the bones I'll break. I count them like rosary beads, a prayer of violence that drowns out Cash's voice.

I think about the photo Eleanor never took—the one with my hands around her son's throat.

The one where his eyes bulge and his tongue turns purple.

The one where I finally become what they always said I was.

I fall into darkness with the words on my lips...

Demon.

For we are many.

The creak of the cabin door wakes me. I crack my eyes open just in time to watch Cash's silhouette disappear into the soft pastel hues of a breaking dawn. Wyatt follows him out. Their voices drop to whispers, but the broken window to my left carries words like the wind.

"This is getting out of hand," Wyatt says, voice tight with something that might be fear. "Marcus is acting crazy, man."

"He's always been a little off," Cash replies.

"No, I mean *crazy* crazy. Says he's keeping Savannah out at north ridge all week."

My muscles lock. North ridge. The hunting cabin. Five miles of pine forest from the main house. No cell service. No neighbors. Just log walls and trophy heads with glass eyes.

And Savannah.

"We're not gonna let him do that, right?" Wyatt's voice cracks. "What if he hurts her?"

I start working the rope again. There's a slickness there. Letting them move smoothly. Blood. My wrists are bleeding.

After a pause that stretches too long, Cash says, "OK. Fine. We'll go check on her. I mean, what is the point of all this if he…"

Cash doesn't finish.

Wyatt asks the same question I'm thinking in my head. "If he what? *Kills her*? You don't think he's gonna kill her, do you? I mean, Cash. What the fuck are we doing? If she's dead…" He stops.

If she's dead… what?

What was he gonna say?

"No," Cash finally responds. "No, we can't have her hurt." Then, quieter, "We need that fucking inheritance."

Inheritance.

What the fuck is happening here?

Is this about my dick inside their sister? Or… something else?

Cash and Wyatt walk out of hearing range, their boots crunching on gravel, voices fading.

There's something off here. This isn't concern for a cherished sister. This isn't brotherly protection.

This is just dollar signs where a heart should be.

The sound of horses being mounted carries through the thin walls. Hoof beats drum the earth, growing distant.

Then it's me and the wilderness.

I keep still, thinking. Trying to sort out all the information I just learned. It doesn't add up. Yet. But it will.

If I can get the fuck out of here.

Mercy.

My sister's name hits like a bullet to the chest. Is she still at the trailer? Did she wake to find me gone? How many times has she already been left? I close my eyes, see her small frame curled on that new bed, BB gun clutched to her chest like a teddy bear. Nine years old and already knows better than to sleep without a weapon.

Did she try calling? Did she think I abandoned her again?

The rope gives another fraction. I twist harder.

Don't give up on me, Mercy. I'm coming home. I swear it.

Savannah's at the north ridge cabin. Marcus is keeping her there. *Cleaning* her. The words twist in my gut like a rusted blade. I've known men like Marcus my whole life—men who think money buys the right to break things. Rich boys who smile for cameras and keep trophies of their sins. Not like normal people. Normal people hurt each other in simple ways. Men like Marcus make art of it.

I pull against the rope, feeling skin tear. Blood trickles warm down my wrists.

What is he doing to her right now? What has he already done?

The rope gives a little more.

Three weeks. That's how long I've been out of prison.

Three fucking weeks of trying to be a man who keeps promises.

Who stays clean.

Who builds instead of burns.

"Never going back to prison," I'd told Mercy. Told myself.

But if Marcus touches Savannah again—if he's already done what Cash implied—I'll kill him slow.

I'll take my time. I'll make sure he feels everything.

And I'll go back to Whitefall with his blood still under my nails.

Another twist. Another tear of skin.

I test the tension in the restraints. Feel the fibers starting to give.

I'm going to walk out of here.

The only question is how much blood it'll take.

Mine. Theirs. Everyone's.

There's a storm building in my chest—not thunder, but something older. Something patient. The kind of violence that doesn't need to announce itself. The kind that simply arrives, like dawn.

Inevitable.
Silent.
Mine.

CHAPTER 3
SAVANNAH

The late afternoon sunlight filters through blinds like dirty prison bars, casting tiger stripes across knotty pine walls that have seen too many men's secrets. I blink against the glare, my head pounding with the kind of ache that feels like someone reached inside and rearranged everything.

The first thing I notice is that the discomfort and fullness of the catheter is gone.

He took it out.

This thought makes me want to throw up.

The invasion.

The violation.

My wrists burn. The zip ties have carved red valleys into my skin while I was sleeping, raw and angry from hours of desperate twisting.

I try to swallow but can't. My tongue feels like sandpaper glued to the roof of my mouth. Whatever drugs Marcus has been forcing into me have left me desert-dry, like all the water's been sucked from my body.

The cup with the bendy straw sits on the nightstand—it's empty. So I must've drank—he must've helped me drink—but I don't remember him returning.

He's been here while I slept. Watching.

The thought makes my skin crawl beneath the restraints. I force myself to push the image of Marcus 'cleaning' me out of my mind.

That's a trauma for another time.

If I get out of here alive, that is.

He's not going to kill me, right?

Surely, he will let me go.

Won't he?

I'm not sure. This isn't the man I knew. That I dated. He's a stranger to me now.

Which is why I can't rely on him being rational. I mean, does a rational man kidnap the Little Ashby Princess?

No. Crazy people do that.

I need to get out of here. I test each binding methodically, starting with my ankles. No give. Left wrist—still tight. Right wrist—

There.

A give. The tiniest weakness in the seal where the ridges lock together.

I freeze, not wanting to damage it further until I have a plan.

The cabin settles around me with familiar creaks as my gaze travels up to the photographs Marcus has arranged like some sick shrine.

They are all watching me now. All these versions of me, trapped behind glass just like I am.

Don't think about that. *Focus.*

I turn my attention back to the tear in the zip tie. It's small, but it's something.

Something is better than nothing when nothing is all you have left.

The door opens with such deliberate slowness that I can count the seconds between the first creak and the full swing.

One-one-thousand. Two-one-thousand.

Like he's savoring my captivity.

Marcus steps inside carrying a pastry box, his smile stretched too wide across his face. When he angles the box onto the bedside table, I can see cherry pie with a perfect lattice crust through the clear plastic window.

"Look who's awake," he says, voice lilting like I'm a child. "I brought my sweetness something sweet."

He's wearing fresh clothes—pressed khakis with a knife-edge crease down the front, blue button-down rolled precisely to mid-forearm. His hair is combed with that perfect political part, not a strand out of place. Meanwhile, I'm filthy with sweat and worse things I don't want to name.

"You must be starving, honey-dove." He's never called me that before. Not once in two years. Where is this all coming from? Did he just... lose his damn mind?

"Time for dessert." Then he winks at me, like he's implying that dessert is something more than cherry pie. "The doctor said you'd be hungry once the sedatives wore off."

Doctor? What doctor?

"I been more rigid with you than I should've been—but the fight in you, Savannah." He draws in a breath through his teeth. "It was unexpected." He puts up a hand. "Not entirely unattractive, though. I like your fight. Oh," he chides. "Don't look so worried, sugar plum. You needn't worry about anything. The world is humming along just fine without you. I've made sure of it."

What the hell does that even mean? I feel like he's hinting at things unsaid. Words that exist between invisible lines.

"I haven't slept in days, just watching over you." His smile never reaches his eyes. They remain flat and calculating, like he's gauging my reactions for a focus group.

"Days?" The word scrapes out of my throat.

"Three, to be exact." He tilts his head. "The healing process takes time. Especially when it's all up in your head."

Three days. My God. I've been here *three days*. I've missed time. Holy fuck, that's an understatement.

Legion feels impossibly far away now. Whatever Cash did to him—it's probably over. He could be—

I can't finish the thought.

My eyes drift to the pie Marcus is serving up for me. That's when I see the embossed Ashby Ranch logo on the side. That means someone from the main house provided this pie. Someone made this pie, packaged it up, and handed it to my kidnapper.

How many people are in on this? Cash, certainly. Wyatt too. Not Colt—he would never. But Aunt Ruth?

The kitchen staff? The ranch hands I've known since childhood?

The betrayal cuts deeper than the zip ties.

All those people who smiled at me, who called me "Miss Savannah" with what I thought was affection—they must hate me.

They must truly hate me to allow this.

To help make it happen.

"Everyone's been so worried about you," Marcus continues, cutting into the pie with a plastic fork. "But I told them you just need time to remember who you really are." He sits on the edge of the bed, his hip pressing against my thigh like a brand. I can't move away. The restraints see to that. "Open wide," he says.

I part my lips and accept the cherry pie without resisting. The longer I stay calm and compliant, the longer I have to come up with a plan. I swallow mechanically, staring at the ceiling beam directly above us.

"You know, when I first realized how deep his hold on you was, I did some research." Marcus hovers a fresh forkful of pie near my lips. "Trauma bonding. Captive identification. It's actually quite common in cases like yours. Naturally, after all those years of manipulation, the detoxification process will take time," he continues. "But the specialist I called from Denver says the symptoms will fade. You'll stop craving his presence once the chemical dependency breaks."

Chemical dependency. Like Legion is some kind of narcotic flowing through my veins, a poison that needs to be purged from my system. Like what we share is a sickness rather than something that's kept me breathing for sixteen years. Marcus speaks about him with clinical detachment, as if describing a particularly aggressive virus that's infected his prize possession.

The fork presses against my closed lips, cherry filling drips slowly onto my chin. Marcus doesn't seem to notice or care, his eyes distant and crazy, just like his mind.

Pretend, the voice in my head says.

Pretend, Savannah. You cannot reason with this man. You need to do everything he says. Give him every reaction he's looking for.

Pretend, even if it kills you.

These last few words are like whispers in a nightmare.

I open my mouth, wrap my lips around the fork, pull the pie off as Marcus withdraws. "Mmmm," I hum. "It's really good, Marcus. Thank you so much for thinking of me. For going all the way back to the ranch to retrieve this special dessert."

Marcus smiles. "Your mother always said you had a sweet tooth." He frowns slightly. narrowing his eyes. "But we mustn't let you get fat, darling. You can't come to campaign events if you're frumpy. So enjoy, for now. But when we get home there will be rules."

Rules. Oh, my god. How the hell did I ever pick this man as a boyfriend, let alone a future husband? What the hell was wrong with me?

Legion wasn't here, I tell myself. He wasn't here to keep my mind straight. To keep me from wandering into the delusions that my life has always been.

And even though I told myself the last time I woke that there's no way that Marcus talked to Eleanor about me—she's been dead for seven years, for fuck's sake—these things he's saying about her ring true.

Like she *might've* told him these things, if she had the chance.

I look up at the ceiling beam again. It's old-growth pine, probably harvested from this very property a century ago. My great-grandfather built this cabin himself. How many secrets has it held? How many Ashby women have stared up at that same beam, trapped in different ways?

Maybe all of them get tied up before marriage? Maybe they all realize, too late, that it's just a trap?

Marcus's thumb drags across the corner of my mouth, lingering longer than necessary to wipe away a smudge of cherry filling. His touch leaves a chill I can't shake.

"Your mother did such an exceptional job raising the perfect political wife," he says, casual as discussing the weather. "I knew it the moment I saw those riding photos from when you were seven. The posture, the poise—you were already being groomed."

Thinking of Marcus studying my childhood like a menu is revolting.

"That first professional photoshoot when you turned nine was particularly inspired," Marcus continues, setting the pie container aside. "Eleanor positioned you on that white pony with the braided mane. You were wearing the blue dress with the eyelet lace collar." His smile doesn't reach his eyes. "It took seventy-eight shots before your mother was satisfied with your smile."

"How do you—"

"Eleanor's journals are quite detailed."

Ho-lee shit.

He's been reading her journals? "I... I didn't even know she had journals."

"No, of course not. They were secret. And part of the sale."

"*Sale*?" I swear, I throw up in my mouth.

"The reason she cataloged you, darling. For me. It was all... *for me*. Our marriage was arranged when you were still in the womb—"

I stop listening. This isn't true. He's lying. Maybe there are journals and that's how he knows these things, but he's lying. Cash found the journals. Or Wyatt. Somehow, Marcus—or his father—got their hands on them.

There is a logical explanation for this!

Right. There is, Savannah. She did this to you. She turned you into... what? A doll? A wife?

Marcus straightens his cuffs. "She documented everything—your diet, your tutors, which friends were acceptable. Even which boys to keep you away from." His mouth twists. "Though she failed spectacularly with Kane."

No, this can't be true. She turned me into a *product*.

Something shatters inside me—not my resolve, but the cloudy glass I've been looking through my entire life. Suddenly everything is razor-sharp, brutally clear.

The carefully staged childhood photos. The protein shakes instead of breakfast when I gained five pounds at thirteen. The "chance" meetings with daughters of state officials that Eleanor orchestrated. The riding lessons not because I loved horses, but because equestrian outfits are... a *fetish*.

My social media empire wasn't my creation at all—it was just the digital continuation of my mother's project. The staged authenticity. The calculated vulnerability. The perfect lighting on supposedly candid moments.

I was never a daughter. I was prepared for market.

Like a fucking steer.

And Marcus isn't my fiancé.

He's my buyer.

I look at him now—really look—and see the same cold calculation I'd glimpsed in my mother's eyes when she'd adjust my chin just so before pressing the shutter. The same proprietary satisfaction when she'd review the perfect shot.

"You've gone quiet," Marcus observes, head tilting. "Are you feeling overwhelmed by my thoughtfulness? I know it's a lot to process—how long I've been preparing to take care of you."

I swallow the acid rising in my throat and force my face to soften. "It's just... surprising," I whisper, making my voice small, grateful. "All this time, you knew me so well."

The words are soft, but inside, my resolve hardens. Not just determination to escape this cabin, this man, these restraints. Something deeper. The resolve to burn "Savannah Ashby" to the ground—the perfect, curated doll they've spent three decades crafting.

If I get out of here alive, that woman dies first.

"Another bite?" Marcus offers, his tone suggesting generosity rather than force.

I accept it, my jaw working mechanically. Cherry juice leaks from the corner of my mouth. His free hand slides up to brush the juice away with his thumb, lingering on my lip. I don't flinch. I've spent twenty-three years being posed, positioned, perfected for cameras. This is just another performance.

"You're being so good today," he says, like I'm a child or a pet. "Much better than yesterday."

I barely even remember yesterday.

Hell, at this point, I barely remember what freedom tastes like.

Is this how it was for Legion? Being locked up in that prison for things he never did? To earn his place in that club? Some stupid patch?

Marcus places the pie container on the nightstand and checks his watch. "Time for your medicine."

"Please," I say, trying to keep the trembling out of my voice. "Marcus, my dear. Can you please let me go to the bathroom."

"Of course, Savannah," He pets my head like I'm a dog. "You didn't respond well to the catheter on the first day, so I've been drugging you just enough to allow you to walk and relieve yourself after eating."

What kind of drugs? How long do I have?

Marcus goes into the bathroom, turns the light on, and I watch as he gets a pill bottle. Twenty minutes, I decide. It will take about twenty minutes to work. Marcus will know this. He will be timing it.

I need to stay awake and lucid. Because this is something far worse than kidnapping.

It's enslavement.

He comes back out, places two white pills on my tongue, and offers me the water glass with the bendy straw.

I sip, try not to swallow them, but they go down anyway.

Stay awake, I tell myself. Over and over in my head. Stay awake. One chance, Stay awake....

"Ready?" Marcus asks. He cuts the zip ties. "Oh..." He chuckles. "This one was nearly broken. Well, we'll double up next time." Come along,"

Stay awake. *Stay awake*.

Marcus helps me up into a sitting position, my eyes swing wildly around the room, searching... searching....

"Let's stand now, sugar-plum."

My feet hit the floor.

I walk.

Stay awake. *Stay awake*.

But the next thing I know, I'm once again waking up in bed.

My bindings tighter than ever.

CHAPTER 4
LEGION

The ropes give another fraction. I can feel the fibers splitting one by one against my raw wrists, each snap a whispered promise. Blood makes for good lubricant when you've got nothin' else.

Life lessons you wish you didn't have to learn so young.

My left wrist is a mess of torn skin and exposed meat. The right isn't much better. But pain's just a message, and I've gotten real good at putting those messages on hold.

The cabin's quiet except for the wind findin' its way through cracks in the old logs that make up the walls. Somewhere outside, a crow calls.

Silence can be a warning all its own.

I need to get out of here.

I twist my wrist again, feeling something tear. My skin or the rope, doesn't matter. Both are coming apart as I work the rope against a splintered edge on the support beam. My shoulders scream from being pulled back at this angle for hours. Feels like my joints are trying to separate.

But it's my only way out of this. So the blood and the pain doesn't matter.

The only thing that matters is escape. Because *he's* got Savannah up at North Ridge. She's with *him*. Even Cash and Wyatt were second-guessing that move.

Don't think about it, Legion, I caution myself.

You can't help her until you're free, so thoughts don't matter. All it'll get you is anger. And anger only works in the desperate end of a fight.

This is not the desperate end of a fight. This is the precarious beginning of a war I never wanted, but will fight to the death anyway.

The thought sends fresh heat through my veins. My right hand curls into a fist, and I feel the rope give another fraction.

Almost there.

I picture Marcus touching her. Hurting her. "Cleaning" her.

"Stay strong, Savannah. I'm coming," I promise this, though no one hears it but the walls.

Another twist. The rope stretches. One more—

There's a sound. Almost musical. The sound of fibers finally surrendering.

My right hand pulls free with a wet slide, arm falling limp at my side. Dead weight. Useless for a minute until the blood starts flowin' back. I grit my teeth against the pins and needles, knowin' what's coming next will hurt worse.

I reach across with clumsy fingers, workin' at the

knots on my left wrist. Each touch feels like I'm digging into my own grave, but I keep going. Keep breathin'.

The left hand comes free, and I lean my head back against the beam. For thirty seconds, I allow myself to just breathe. To feel how close I came to never getting up again.

Then I'm moving.

I crawl first, then stagger to my feet. My legs are weak from sitting so long, and the cabin spins. But I find the wall and steady myself against the rough-cut logs.

Cash's boot did some damage. Each breath bubbles something wet in my chest. I spit blood onto the floor, adding to the mess I've already made.

"Not dying here," I tell the empty room. "Not today."

I make it to the door and I'm just about to pull it open, when the sound of hoof beats hits my ears.

Fuck.

I took thirty seconds too long. That break, thirty seconds, might be what stands between life and death today.

I grab an old piece of wood lying by the collapsed fireplace, slide up to the wall, lean my back against the logs, and wait.

The door swings open. Wood creaks, and when the golden hour of light floods in, I don't hesitate.

I lunge from my position, swinging the broken piece of lumber with everything I've got left. My body screams in protest, ribs grinding against each other like they're trying to puncture whatever's left of my lungs.

"Fuck—!" A voice shouts as my makeshift weapon

connects. Not as solid as I wanted, but enough to send the intruder stumbling backward.

"Wait! Legion! I came to help!"

Colt Ashby. The pretty one. The one who wasn't there last night.

Doesn't matter. He's still an Ashby.

I tackle him to the ground, ignoring the wet crack in my chest. We hit hard, and I'm on top of him, blood from my wrists dripping onto his expensive shirt. His face is all wide eyes and shock beneath me.

"You fucking Ashbys," I snarl, pushing my forearm into his throat. "Think you own everything. Everyone. This is one fuck up too many."

He tries to speak, but I'm pressing too hard. Good. Let him feel what it's like not to breathe. Let him know what it feels like when someone decides your life isn't worth shit.

"It wasn't me," he chokes out when I ease up just enough. "I've been out of town. Ranch hand called—told me what happened."

I study his face, looking for the lie. His eyes are clear. Panicked, but not deceitful.

"Then what the hell are you doing here?" My voice is a low growl, barely human.

"Because this is wrong," he chokes, and there's something in his voice that sounds like the truth. "I came to help. Marcus has lost his mind. Cash and Wyatt crossed a line."

I ease back, just a fraction. Just enough that he can take a full breath.

"You're still a piece of shit," I tell him, standing slowly, feeling every broken rib shift under my skin.

"You're a dirty fucking piece of shit Ashby! Do you have any goddamn idea what they're doing to Savannah right now? What your own blood is letting happen to her while you've been conveniently out of town?"

Colt sits up, rubbing his throat, choking out words. "Outside. Three horses. One for each of us."

"Each of us?"

"You, me, and Savannah." He tries to get up, but pauses to cough first.

I do not feel guilty.

Once he rightens himself, he nods toward the door. "We need to go. *Now*. Cash and Wyatt will be coming back. There was a delivery at the ranch they needed to take care of, but it won't take long. They're probably already on their way."

None of that sounds good.

"Cash said Marcus was keeping her at North Ridge," I say, watching his reaction.

"I know where she is." Colt backs up with his hands out like he's warding me off. "They told me everything. Marcus has been keeping her sedated for three days now."

Three days.

The words hit me like another boot to the chest. Three fucking days I've been tied to that post while Savannah's been—

No. Don't think about it. Not yet.

My blood turns to ice in my veins. Cold. Focused. This isn't rage anymore. This is something deeper. "If you're lying to me," I say, my voice so calm it scares even me, "I will peel the skin from your bones. Slowly. While you watch."

Colt nods, looking me straight in the eyes. "I know. I know, Legion. Trust me, I know."

There's somethin' about the way he says my name. Something… I dunno. Real in it.

"You don't know shit," I tell him. "You don't know me at all, Colt Ashby. What you think you know isn't even a fraction of the raging hell I'm capable of."

We stare at each other for a few moments. Long enough that I notice… he and Savanah have the same eyes.

"Noted," he says. "I'm here to help, Legion. Just like the other night, remember? I left the gate open. I let you in to the engagement party. I made it happen. We're not enemies, Legion. We're not."

It's true. He did let me in. I saw him in Terry that first week I was out. I didn't even ask to be let in, either. He offered. Why would he do that?

"It wasn't for me," I say.

"No," he agrees. "It wasn't for you. It was for Savannah. She was dyin' without you, Legion. Dyin'. And this Marcus fuck… I can't stand that asshole. Maybe you and I aren't friends, but we're not enemies, either. We both want the same thing right now. Get Savannah home safe."

I scoff. "Home safe? This *is* home, Colt. She's already *home*. Home isn't safe. Not with a bunch of psychopaths runnin' things."

Colt's shoulders drop. Like he was holding in this judgement and suddenly decided to let it go. He knows it's true. Savannah isn't safe here anymore. "Let's just go get her." Then he turns and walks out.

I follow him out into the dusky evening, each step a

negotiation between pain and necessity. My ribs are screamin', my head is thumpin', and the late afternoon sun burns my eyes after days in that dark cabin. My vision swims, but I force myself to focus.

Three horses stand tethered to a nearby pine. I recognize Cassia instantly—Savannah's mare. The sight of her makes something twist in my chest that isn't just broken ribs.

Colt reaches into his saddlebag and pulls out two guns. He hands me one, and I immediately check the chamber, the weight familiar in my hand. Then I notice what he's holding.

"What the fuck is that?" I demand.

"Tranquilizer gun." He says it like it's the most reasonable thing in the world.

"A fucking tranq gun? Are you serious?" I stare at him, incredulous. "Your sister's been kidnapped by some psycho politician's son, and you brought a goddamn dart gun?"

"We're not killing anyone, for fuck's sake." Colt's voice rises. "We're rescuing someone. Marcus can be put out. He's the senator's son—we can't *kill* him."

I feel something shift inside me. A door opening to a room I promised myself I'd keep locked. But promises are just words, and words don't mean shit when someone you love is bleeding.

"Watch me," I say, each word dropping like stone.

"Legion—"

"No." I cut him off. "You don't get it. Three days, Colt. Three fucking days she's been up there with him. If he's touched her, I'm going to cut off his fingers one by one. Make him eat them. Then I'll open his stomach so he can see them sitting there."

Colt's face pales, but I can't stop. The images come too fast, too vivid.

"Maybe I'll start with his eyes. Scoop them out with a spoon so he feels every second. Feed them to the crows while he listens." My voice doesn't even sound like mine anymore. It's the voice from The Pit. The one that kept me alive when they tried to break me. "Or I could just skin him. Slow. Strip by strip. Salt each piece before starting the next."

"Jesus Christ, Legion."

"You think that's bad?" I laugh, and it's a sound that belongs in a nightmare. "I haven't even gotten creative yet. I could—"

"Enough!" Colt snaps. "This isn't helping Savannah."

Her name pulls me back. Just enough to remember why we're here.

"Listen," Colt says, "There's more to this story than you know about."

"Oh fuck you, Ashby. But yeah," I narrow my eyes down at him. "There's a *lot* fuckin' more to this story. Shit that would turn your insides sour if you knew."

Colt loses some color in his face, but he recovers quick—meeting my gaze straight on. "You think I don't know that? Why the fuck do you think I'm here?"

"Because you got a conscience? Little fucking late for that." I spit blood onto the dirt between us. "Three years late."

"I'm not Cash," he says, checking the tranquilizer gun. "And I'm not Wyatt. I've been planning this for a long time."

"Planning what?" My fingers tighten around the gun he gave me.

"Getting away from them. All of them." He looks up at the mountain where Savannah's being held. "There's something you need to know about—" But he suddenly quits talking.

"About what," I sneer. "What the fuck are you talking about?"

"Let me just say this, " Colt replies, his voice just as low and threatening as mine. "This isn't just Cash being a protective brother. It's not just Marcus being a jealous fiancée. It's fucking business, Legion."

"She's not property," I growl.

"To them, she *is*. Savannah is the key to forty-seven thousand acres of Ashby land. This is an *empire*, Legion. A legitimate American dynasty on the line here and Savannah has control of all of it. Every fucking square inch. Water rights are worth more than gold, you know that much." He looks me dead in the eye. "You think they're going to let her run off with some ex-con biker because she's in *love*, Legion? Fuck no. They'll break her first."

My knuckles go white around the gun. "I'll kill them all."

"And end up back in prison, leaving Savannah with no one." Colt shakes his head. "That's exactly what they want. Why do you think they let you out a day early? Why did Cash pick you up instead of your club?"

"To fuck with me."

"To *isolate* you. Set you up. They've been playing chess this whole time. It's all been planned." Then he pauses. And this pause here is what makes me go pale now. Because he finishes up with, "You don't even know the half of it."

We stare at each other for a few moments, all three horses getting anxious. Stomping their feet.

Colt cuts away first, swings up onto his horse. "You're out of your depth here, Kane. You need my help. I'm not asking you to be nice about it or even grace me with a fuckin' thank you because Savannah is *my sister*. *My* blood. And we both know how you'd act if it was your blood on the line. You'd forgive an ex-con biker if your sister loved him."

I don't say anything back because… he's right. But I don't want to admit that either, so—

"Can you even *ride*, Legion?" Colt asks, sneering down his nose at me from atop his horse.

I spit blood into the dirt. "I'll fuckin' manage."

Then I swing up too, he grabs Cassia's lead, and we bolt down the mountain.

The horses move like ghosts beneath us, silent across Ashby land. Colt leads, I follow, my body a temple of pain and my mind a slaughterhouse of revenge. Every step jolts my broken ribs. Every heartbeat pounds inside my head.

The north ridge rises against the twilight, a black shape cutting into purple sky. The cabin sits nestled in pines, windows glowing yellow.

"No horses," Colt whispers as we dismount. "Cash and Wyatt aren't here."

Good. Two less bodies to put in the ground.

We tie the horses. My hands shake—not from fear

but from something darker. Something rising. I've spent three years in a cage learning to control it, but now I feel the lock breaking.

"Legion," Colt grabs my arm. "Remember what I said."

I shake him off without agreeing to shit.

We don't waste time with stealth. The door splinters under our combined weight, wood cracking like bones. Inside, the smell hits first—antiseptic, sweat, and something medicinal.

And there she is.

Savannah lies on a bed, wrists bound with plastic ties cutting into flesh. Her eyes are wide, unfocused, drugged but on the verge of alert. Her dress—the same one from the silo—is wrinkled and stained.

Marcus stands over her with a fucking syringe.

Our eyes lock. His widen with recognition, then fear.

"You're not supposed to be—"

I don't let him finish. My body becomes a weapon, launched across the room. I hit him with the force of every dark day in Whitefall, every night I dreamed of her voice, every second she's been in this nightmare.

We crash to the floor. Something snaps beneath us—his arm, maybe his collarbone. The sound feeds something primal in me.

My fist connects with his face. Once. Twice. A third time. Each impact sends blood spattering across the floor. His nose caves. His cheek splits. His teeth crack against my knuckles.

"Legion!" Colt's voice sounds miles away.

I keep hitting. Four. Five. Six. Blood slicks my hands,

warm and satisfying. I feel nothing but the rhythm of destruction. Seven. Eight.

"This is for touching her," I growl, landing another blow. "This is for drugging her." Another. "This is for thinking you own her."

The next hit lands with a wet crunch. Marcus gurgles beneath me, face unrecognizable. Something in my chest breaks open—not a rib, but something deeper.

The demon they named me for, clawing its way out.

"*LEGION!*" Colt's voice cuts through the red fog. "*THINK ABOUT SAVANNAH!*"

I pause, fist raised, blood dripping between my fingers. I turn to see her watching, eyes glassy but fixed on me.

There's a soft pop and hiss. Marcus's body goes slack beneath me as Colt's tranquilizer dart finds its mark in his thigh.

"Get off him," Colt hisses, pulling at my shoulder. "He's done. Look at *her*. Look at Savannah."

Her name breaks through. I push off Marcus, leaving him crumpled on the floor, face a ruin of blood and bone. Still breathing. The senator's son lives.

For now.

I move to the bed, finding a scalpel on a metal tray beside it. The sight of it—clean, precise, meant for her skin—makes bile rise in my throat. I use it to slice through the zip ties binding her wrists.

Her skin is raw underneath, bleeding in places where she fought against the restraints. Bruises circle her ankles. Her lip is split at the corner. But her eyes—they find mine, recognition flickering through the drug haze.

"Legion," she whispers, voice cracked from disuse or screaming. I don't want to know which.

"I'm here." I gather her up, one arm under her knees, one supporting her back. She weighs nothing. "I've got you."

She starts to cry then, silent tears tracking down her face. Each one feels like a knife between my ribs as I carry her from that room.

"We're leaving," I murmur against her hair, keeping my voice low and steady despite the rage still burning through me. "You're okay now. I've got you. Nobody's gonna touch you again."

Outside, the night air hits us. Clean. Cold. Real.

I lift her onto Cassia, who stands perfectly still, like she knows. Savannah's fingers curl weakly into the mare's mane.

"Can you hold on?" I ask her.

She nods, eyes clearer now, like the fresh air is burning away some of the fog. I mount my own horse, muscles screaming in protest.

Colt appears, his horse jogging excitedly. "We need to move. Now."

We start down the mountain, away from the cabin where Marcus lies bleeding but alive. Away from the nightmare. Toward my trailer, toward something like safety.

But the demon in me isn't satisfied.

It wants to go back.

Wants to finish what I started.

And part of me knows I have woken something up that I can't put back to sleep.

. . .

We ride through darkness, three shadows cuttin' across Ashby land. The horses' hooves beat a rhythm like war drums against packed earth. Savannah slumps forward on Cassia, leaning onto her neck. Her fingers white-knuckled in the mare's mane. Her breathing comes shallow. Too shallow.

Cassia steps carefully. Like she knows.

The trailer appears over the ridge, no lights on.

I dismount first, legs nearly buckling. My ribs scream, but I ignore them, reaching up for Savannah. She falls into my arms like something broken, all the fight gone from her limbs. Her skin feels cold despite the summer night.

Colt stays mounted, gathering the reins of my horse. He promises to handle his brothers, says something about buying us time. I barely hear him. The world has narrowed to the weight of her against my chest and the way her breath hitches when I shift her.

He tells Savannah to stay with me for now, that he'll make this right.

Empty words from an Ashby. But he takes the horses, snapping lead ropes to their bridles and securing them to his saddle, and then he's gone—hoofbeats fadin' into the desert like distant thunder.

I put Savannah down and help her inside, she stumbles through as I kick the door shut behind us. My hand finds the shotgun I keep mounted by the entrance, I check it's loaded, then slide the deadbolt home.

The demon in me still burns for blood. For Marcus's throat beneath my hands. For Cash's skull cracking against stone. For every man who touched her, drugged her, thought they owned her. The rage sits in my chest like something living, something starved.

Savannah leans against the kitchen counter, swayin' on her feet. The movement draws my eyes to her—really see her. Her wrists raw meat where the zip ties bit. Bruises blooming on her arms like dark flowers. Her lip split. Her eyes vacant from whatever they pumped into her veins.

Something cracks inside me. Not the demon breaking free, but something worse. Something that feels like drowning.

She looks up, her gaze finding mine through the haze. She tries to say something, but the words won't come.

I set the shotgun down as Savannah places her hands on the counter. Her eyes catch on something I missed—a piece of paper. She lifts it with trembling fingers, holds it up like evidence.

I walk over and take it. The handwriting hits before the words do. Diesel's chicken scratch, all hard angles and impatience.

WHERE THE HELL ARE YOU?

"Mercy," I breathe. I lunge for the landline mounted on the kitchen wall, my fingers trembling as I punch in the clubhouse number. Three rings. Four. Each one stretching time like torture.

"Yeah." Diesel's voice, gravel and cigarettes.

"It's me," I say, voice steadier than my insides. "Where's—"

"Is that Legion?" A small, sleepy voice cuts through the background.

The tension drains from my shoulders so fast I nearly drop the phone. "Let me talk to her."

"Nah." Diesel's voice hardens. "You got some explainin' to do first, brother. You've been missing for three fucking days. Where the fuck are you? Brick's been patient, we all have. Took the kid in. But this shit ends now. We got people here, product moving. Ya understand?"

"I get it," I say, lowering my voice. "Shit went down here. I'll explain—"

"What shit?" Diesel growls.

I look at Savannah, bruised and drugged against my counter. At the shotgun I set down. At the blood still drying under my fingernails.

"They kidnapped us, Diesel. We just got free."

"What? Who?" He's bellowing. "Who the fuck kidnapped you?"

"I'll be there," I say, each word measured. "Soon as I can. And I'll tell ya everythin'. It's too much for the phone and I need to take care of Savannah. She's been drugged for three days."

Then I hang up, not waiting for his answer, not interested in his approval.

This goes way beyond club business.

This is personal.

I guide Savannah to the bathroom, one arm around her waist like she's made of smoke that might scatter in a breeze. The drugs are still inside her, makin' her movements slow and dreamlike. She doesn't flinch when I flip the light on, doesn't blink at the sudden brightness. That scares me more than the bruises.

I turn the shower knob all the way left, hot as it'll go. Steam rises, filling the small space between us.

"Let me," I whisper, reaching for the hem of her torn dress.

She lifts her arms like a child. The fabric comes away, and there it is—the evidence. Bruises blooming across her ribs, her thighs. Fingerprints pressed into her skin like they were trying to claim her from the inside out. The zip tie burns around her wrists, raw and angry. I catalog each mark, each wound. File them away with the debt I'll collect later.

The demon in my chest paces behind my ribs, hungry for blood. I breathe through it. Not now. Not here.

She stands naked before me, our eyes meetin'. But there's nothing sexual in it. Just broken things recognizing each other.

I shed my own clothes, wincing as dried blood pulls at new scabs, then guide her under the spray. She gasps as the hot water hits her skin, the first real sound she's made since we got here.

I let her stand in the water as I wash her hair. Long, careful strokes. Rinse. Condition. Like I'm putting something precious back together. She leans into my hands, eyes closed. I wash her body next, gentle over the bruises, gentler over the places Marcus touched. Like I could wash him away if I just try hard enough.

She kisses me first. Reaches up, pulls my face down to hers. She tastes broken. Her fingers find the brand on my chest—the Badlands 'B' red and swollen against my skin. She traces it, questions in her touch.

"It means family," I say, voice low against her ear. "Could be yours too, if you want it." My fingers brush her cheek. "The club protects what's mine, and you—" I press my forehead to hers, "—you're the most mine thing I've ever had."

Steam clouds around us, thick enough to hide in. Her body trembles against mine, but not from cold. From need. From something neither of us can name.

"I need you," she whispers, her voice cracking on the words.

"I need you too," I say, because a truer thing has never been said.

"No, Legion." She breathes heavy. Labored. Looks up at me. "I need *you*. Inside me."

"Savannah, I don't—"

Her fingertips on my lips stop the objection. "Shh," she says. "Please don't argue with me. You don't understand. He…"

"He what?" I growl. She doesn't answer. "Did he rape you?"

Her head shakes and relief floods through me.

"He… cleaned me, Legion. I don't even know what that means, but…" Her eyes plead with me. "He left a mark. Some kind of mark on me. And water isn't enough to chase it away. I need *you*."

Now it makes sense. She needs me to erase him. To be inside her so she can forget about whatever he did.

I understand this is not a fix. It's a cope.

But I can't deny that I need it too. To claim her as mine again.

My hands slide down her sides, mapping the

bruises, memorizing each one. I lift her up like she weighs nothing, pressing her back against the tiled wall. Her legs wrap around my waist, ankles crossing behind me. The brand on my chest burns where it touches her skin.

"Tell me if I hurt you," I murmur against her throat.

She shakes her head, water droplets falling from her hair. "You can't."

I line myself up and push inside her, slow and steady. She's tight, slick, perfect. Her breath catches, a small sound that cuts through the steam and water. I hold still, buried to the root, our bodies locked together.

"Fuck," I breathe against her ear. "Feel how good we fit? Like you were made for me."

Her fingers dig into my shoulders, nails leaving marks in my skin. "Move," she commands, the drugs making her voice raw. "Please."

I do. Slow, deep strokes that make her gasp with each one. No rush. No hurry. Just us, finding our way back to each other through the hurt. The water runs down my back, between us where we're joined. Her head falls back against the tile, eyes half-closed, mouth open.

"That's it," I encourage, my voice a growl. "Take what you need."

She tightens around me, walls clenching. "Legion," she moans, the sound of my name on her lips better than any prayer.

I thrust deeper, harder, but still measured. Still in control. Her legs tighten around me, pulling me closer. The bruises on her thighs press against my hips, but she doesn't wince. Doesn't pull away.

"You're mine," I whisper against her throat. "Say it."

"Yours," she gasps, nails digging deeper. "Always yours."

CHAPTER 5
SAVANNAH

I feel nothing but Legion—inside me, around me, holding me up when my legs have gone liquid. When it's over, I press my forehead against his shoulder, breathing in steam, and copper, and him.

"Stay with me," he murmurs, mistaking my silence for the drugs pulling me under again.

"I'm here," I whisper, though I'm not sure where here is anymore. Not the Savannah who wears diamonds. Not the Savannah who smiles for cameras. Just... raw. Unfiltered. Stripped down to bone and breath.

Legion carries me from the shower, sets me on the closed toilet lid, wraps a towel around my shoulders. Not the Egyptian cotton I'm used to, but somehow softer. He doesn't speak while he dries my hair with another towel, his touch gentle like I'm something that might break.

"We need to go," he says finally, his voice low. "I've got clothes you can wear."

I nod, watching him open the medicine cabinet. He

takes out gauze, medical tape, a tube of antibiotic ointment. I stare at the brand on his chest. An angry red B surrounded by blistered, weeping skin.

It's infected. Anyone can see that.

He follows my gaze, touches the edge of the burn with his fingertips. "It's fine."

It's not fine. Nothing about that thing is fine.

It's deliberate mutilation.

What makes a man allow other men to burn their mark into his flesh like he's cattle? Like he's property?

Course, I don't say any of this out loud. What right do I have? I let my mother photograph every private moment of my childhood. I let Marcus believe he owned me.

Legion quickly dresses the wound, wincing the whole time. Then he gives my wrists and ankles the same treatment.

I was tied to a bed. I was violated. Not as bad as it could've been, but that's like saying drowning is better than burning. Either way, something precious gets taken.

"This might sting," Legion murmurs, dabbing ointment on the raw circles where the zip ties bit into my skin. His hands are steady, but his jaw keeps clenching, unclenching. Little earthquakes of rage he's trying to contain.

"How long was I there?" My voice sounds strange to my own ears. Sandpaper wrapped in cotton.

"Three days." Legion's fingers pause on my wrist, his thumb brushing over my pulse point. "What do you remember?"

Flashes. Marcus's voice, sticky-sweet like syrup left

too long in the sun. The smell of cherry pie. The drugs making the world tilt sideways. His hands on me, washing places that weren't his to touch.

"Enough," I whisper. "Not everything."

Maybe that's a blessing.

Maybe it's worse not knowing.

Legion leaves for a moment before coming back with clothes. White t-shirt with some kind of picture on it that's faded nearly to nothing. Jeans, soft but too big and too long. And a hoodie - black with the Badlands name splashed across the front. "I don't have no shoes for you," he says. "I only have the one pair of boots—no time for shopping these days. And Mercy's shoes are too small. But you'll be OK, right? Until we can get you settled?"

I nod. Shoes are the least of my worries.

He helps me dress, careful not to brush against the bruises blooming like ink stains across my ribs. All of it is too big, but I'm instantly warm. Wearing Legion's clothes is like being hugged by him and it all smells like leather and smoke and something darker.

"They're gonna be looking for us," he says, pulling on jeans. No underwear. I watch the denim slide up his thighs, catching on still-damp skin. "They'll look here first. So we're goin' to the clubhouse. Mercy's there. We'll go there too, figure out next steps."

The clubhouse. Where men with knives, and guns, and criminal records drink, and fight ,and plan whatever men like that plan.

Where they branded Legion like property.

"Marcus will call his father," I say, the words tasting sour. "Senator White has friends in the police. He'll call

Cash and Wyatt. They'll say I'm unstable, that I need to be brought home for my own safety."

Legion's face hardens. "You're not going back."

"I know that," I snap, sharper than I meant to. "But they have resources we don't."

He steps right up to me, hands on my face. His palms are callused, warm. "The club has resources too, Savannah. Different kind, but just as effective."

I want to believe him. I want to believe we can outrun this—my family, Marcus, the carefully constructed cage they've built around me since birth. But I've spent thirty years being Savannah Ashby, and I know better.

"I'm tired," I say instead of arguing. "Can we just... go?"

Legion nods, helping me walk. My legs feel disconnected from my body, like I'm a marionette with half the strings cut. He steadies me with an arm around my waist.

"I need to grab some things first," he says.

I lean against the wall in the hallway while he moves through the trailer, gathering what we need. Through the small window, I can see the moon rising over the prairie, painting everything silver-white. The same view I've seen my whole life, just from a different angle.

Once he's got what he needs, he shrugs on his leather cut—the vest with patches that marks him as Badlands. Property of. Member of. Belonging to. Then the jacket. All black leather and zippers. Covered in Club patches that document a life I know almost nothing about.

We step outside into the night air that smells like coming rain. His motorcycle sits under the porch light, waiting like a black matte beast. Legion hands me his helmet—he's only got one—and I take it and put it on as he swings his leg over and kicks the bike to life.

The engine growls, hungry.

Legion nods to me. I climb behind him and wrap my arms around his waist. The bike roars beneath us, vibration climbing up through my bones as we pull away from the trailer, away from what just happened in the cabin, away from the person I was three days ago.

The highway unfolds like black ribbon, just moonlight to guide us. Wind cuts across my neck where the hoodie doesn't cover. I press myself against Legion's back, arms tight around him. His hand finds mine, squeezes once, then returns to the handlebar.

The drugs still fog the edges of my mind, but the night air and the rumble between my thighs burns some of it away.

I hold tighter to Legion's jacket, feeling the patches under my fingers.

Wondering what I'm riding toward.

Wondering what I've left behind as Legion takes me away from the only life I've ever known. Barefoot on the back of a Harley doing seventy on a Montana back road. The pegs are cold against my soles, and every bump jars my bruises like fruit in a basket.

I left whatever was left of Savannah Ashby, ranch princess, back in that cabin.

What I am now is a girl in borrowed clothes with asphalt grit between her toes.

After what seems like a long time of nothing but

wind, we turn off the highway onto a dirt road. The bike kicks up dust that fills my mouth and coats my skin.

We slow as a chain-link fence appears, topped with barbed wire that catches the moonlight like fish hooks. Floodlights cut through the darkness, illuminating spray-painted words across a metal gate: NO MERCY, NO MASTERS.

A figure emerges from shadows—lanky, nervous hands. He slides the gate open without a word, and Legion nods as we pass through. The young man's eyes catch on me, widen, then drop away quick.

The clubhouse sprawls before us at the end of a dust-packed main street, a two-story structure built from weathered timber and corrugated steel. The front porch stretches the length of the building, its boards sun-bleached and warped. Heavy wooden doors the color of brown rust host the club emblem—a skull wrapped in barbed wire.

Rows of motorcycles gleam in formation, chrome and black, lined up like soldiers. The building hulks against the night sky, more bunker than home.

But this *is* home to Legion. I can feel it in how his shoulders relax, how his breathing changes.

Legion cuts the engine, kicks the stand, and silence rushes in. He swings his leg over, then helps me off. My legs wobble, still weak from whatever they pumped into me. His hands take off my helmet, then steady my waist.

For a moment it's just us, breathing together in the dark.

Then they appear.

Men materialize from doorways, from shadows, from around corners. Big men with hard eyes and leather cuts like Legion's. A few women hover at the edges, but an older lady with silver hair down to her waist waves them back inside. Her eyes catch mine, measuring, judging.

"Legion!" A small voice cuts through the tension. Mercy barrels across the lot, all knobby knees and flying hair. "You left me! You said you wouldn't leave me again!"

Legion catches her, lifts her up against his chest. "I know, Merce. I'm sorry."

"You promised," she says, pounding tiny fists against his shoulders. "You promised!"

Then Mercy sees me. Her fists stop mid-air. "Savannah?"

The silence shifts. Every pair of eyes turns to me—really looks at me. At my dead eyes. At Legion's clothes hanging off my frame. At my bare feet on the cracked blacktop.

Little stones dig into my soles. The collective gaze of a biker gang weighs on my skin, heavier than any camera my mother ever pointed at me.

"I've got no shoes," I say, because it's all I can think to say.

Something in the air changes. The edges of everything go soft. The silver-haired woman's face shifts from suspicion to something else.

"Mercy, go on up to bed," she says, her voice surprisingly gentle.

"But—"

"Now, honey. Go on."

She does. She leaves. But something else remains.

I can't really put my finger on it, it's more of... an aesthetic. Something gloomy and gray. Something... woeful remains behind.

I've complicated things.

I've ruined Legion's homecoming.

Now they all just look sad, these dangerous men with their tattooed knuckles and knife scars.

Legion bends suddenly, scoops me into his arms like I weigh nothing. My head rests against his chest, right over the infected brand that marks him as theirs.

He kisses my cheek, smiles at me with a gentleness that doesn't reach his eyes. "You're OK," he tells me, though we both know that's a lie. "I've got you now."

Then he carries me inside, past the ring of watchful outlaws, into the dark heart of the Badlands where a neon skull sign flickers blue-white-blue against the far wall.

Legion's arms are steady beneath me, but my thoughts scatter like prairie birds. Tryin' to see everything at once. This room isn't just a bar, though it has one—long and gleaming with bottles that catch the neon's pulse. It's something more.

Couches line the walls, worn leather cracked in places that tell stories of men too drunk to stand.

A pool table dominates the center. Video games—the old kind with joysticks and pixelated screens—stand sentinel in the corner like artifacts from another time.

Every surface tells a story I wasn't meant to hear.

Everyone follows us in, silent as church. Their boots make less noise than they should on these old boards. One steps forward from the pack. Older, with eyes like winter and a beard that's seen more summers than I have birthdays.

Legion says, "Brick." Like that's enough. Like evoking his name is an explanation all its own. The name fits—he's built like something that could crush you without trying.

Brick doesn't look at me. He points to something across the room—a door, maybe, or another hallway—but his eyes stay locked on Legion.

"Now," he says. Just that. One word that hangs in the air like smoke.

Legion nods, understanding something I don't. He moves to a couch with faded paisley upholstery and sets me down gently, like I might break.

I might, actually. I'm not sure yet.

He crouches in front of me, his eyes finding mine. There's a softness there that doesn't match the rest of this place, or these people.

"I'll be right back," he says, voice low enough that only I can hear. "You stay right here—no one will fuck with you. All right?"

I realize I'm still clutching his motorcycle helmet against my chest like it's the only thing keeping me together. Maybe it is. My knuckles have gone white around the edges.

Legion smiles, just barely, and brushes a piece of hair from my eyes. His fingers linger against my temple, and I lean into the touch without meaning to. The brand on his chest must hurt, but he doesn't show it.

"OK?" he asks again, searching my face.

I nod because speaking feels impossible. My throat's

gone dry, and the words that used to come so easily—the perfect captions for perfect photos—have abandoned me.

What would I say anyway?

I'm scared. I'm lost. I don't know these people. I don't know myself anymore.

His thumb brushes my cheek one more time, and then he stands. The space between us suddenly feels vast and cold.

I hold the helmet tighter.

CHAPTER 6
LEGION

I push through the door to Brick's office with my ribs screaming at me to stop moving. The taste of my own blood lingers on my tongue, a familiar reminder of consequences.

The room goes quiet.

Five men, five cuts, five pairs of eyes taking in the damage.

The fluorescent light buzzes overhead, casting harsh shadows across weathered faces and battle-scarred knuckles.

Nobody asks if I'm okay.

That's not how this works.

Questions about pain are for civilians, for people who haven't chosen this life. Inside these walls, wounds are just evidence of commitment.

I plant my boots on the hardwood floor, shoulders carrying the weight of my cut that feels heavier than usual.

"Savannah stays," I say, voice rough, but absolutely

resolute. "Forty-eight hours. Inside these walls. Under my cut and my personal guard."

Not a request or a suggestion—a statement of fucking fact.

I don't really have the right to make this demand, but I do it anyway.

The club hierarchy has rules, chains of command that don't bend for personal vendettas or old flames, but Savannah's place here needs to be established immediately.

As in, *right fucking now*, before anyone has time to think about what her presence means.

Brick doesn't move from behind his desk. Just fixes me with those ice-chip eyes that haven't blinked since I walked in. His fingers rest on the scarred wood, steady as stone. The silence stretches like a rubber band about to snap, tension building in the stale air that reeks of cigarettes, gun oil, and old leather.

Then everyone talks at once.

"You bring her straight here? Any trackers? Burner phones?" Roach paces the three steps his lanky frame allows in the cramped space. His fingers twitch like they're looking for a trigger, nervous energy radiating off him in waves. "Those Ashby fuckers got resources. Satellite. Private security. They could be—"

"Unbudgeted liability." Ledger slams his ledger book closed. The sound cracks through the room like a gunshot. His glasses catch the light as he glares at me over the rims. "A fucking Ashby on our property? You know what that costs us? In legal exposure alone—"

"Gate's soft tonight." Havoc doesn't look at me, just stares at the map on the wall, fingers tracing invisible routes across the terrain he knows better than his own face. "Two prospects, green as grass. If Ashby riders show up, we're fifteen minutes from full strength, minimum."

Diesel says nothing. Just moves three steps to stand at my back, arms crossed over his chest like steel beams. I feel the shift in the room's gravity.

Whatever else these men think about me bringing Savannah here, my sergeant at arms has just made his position clear.

Blood for blood, brother for brother.

My ribs throb with each heartbeat, a metronome of pain keeping time with my racing thoughts. The brand on my chest feels like it's burning all over again, the memory of the hot iron and pledged loyalty searing through skin and muscle.

But I start talking because everyone's nervous and no one needs that. In this room, fear is contagious, and right now, I need these men steady, not spooked. So I take a slow breath and let the pain keep me focused and present. I need that now more than ever—this sharp, relentless reminder that I'm still here, still standing despite everything this world has tried to do to break me.

"Let me spell out what happened." My voice stays level, quiet even. Not because I'm calm—because I'm so fucking far beyond rage that I've circled back to something that looks like peace. It's that dangerous stillness that comes when you've passed through the fire and emerged as something harder, colder, more focused than before.

"Savannah and I were having sex out at this silo

where we always hook up. Cash, Wyatt, and Marcus White Jr.—Senator White's son—showed up with ranch hands. They beat me until I couldn't stand, kidnapped me, and tied me to a support beam in a hunting cabin. Savannah—"

I have to stop, swallow the blood that's pooling under my tongue. The metallic taste floods my mouth, bringing back memories of The Pit, of fights where I learned to keep going even when my body begged to quit.

"Marcus took her to another cabin on the Ashby land. Kept her tied to a bed for three days. Drugged her. Did things I'm still putting together."

The room goes still.

Even Roach stops fidgeting.

The air changes, thickens with a tension I recognize —the collective rage of men who understand exactly what I'm not saying, who know what happens to women in cabins where no one can hear them scream.

"Colt Ashby broke ranks. Got me out. Brought horses." I press my palm against my side where something's definitely broken inside. Each breath sends jagged shards of pain through my ribs, but I keep my face blank, unreadable. "We rode to the cabin where Savannah was. Found Marcus standing over her with a syringe. I beat him until Colt pulled me off and shot him with a tranq gun."

Havoc nods once, his eyes meeting mine. He understands exactly what I'm not saying. He knows what I did to Marcus so far has nothing to do with what I will still do to him when this is all over.

"We didn't have no phones on us. So no one tracked us that way. We didn't have any vehicles, we crossed Ashby land on horseback. So they didn't track us that way either. We went straight to the trailer and I made exactly one call on the landline." I point to the floor beneath us, to the clubhouse that's become more home than the trailer ever was. "I called *here*. Colt took the horses back to the ranch and told me he was gonna handle his brothers."

"And the senator's son?" Brick finally speaks, each word measured like expensive whiskey, poured with deliberate precision. His steel eyes track every twitch of my face, reading the truth beneath my words.

"Alive." The word tastes like failure. "No bodies. No murder charges. No federal spotlight on Badlands before the next gun run."

Ledger snorts, tapping his pen against the desk. The rhythmic click-click-click counts down the seconds until my fate is decided. "Alive doesn't mean whole. What's the tangible cost to us? Hard numbers."

I reach into my pocket, fingers finding the rubber-banded stack that Brick handed me just weeks ago. Prison payout. New life money. The cash that was meant to give me and Mercy a fresh start away from everything we came from.

I peel the rubber band off and place the stack on the desk with steady hands that don't betray how much this costs me.

"You guys can take whatever's left of my stack. Dock whatever you need for security costs, additional men, whatever fines the club sees fit." I don't blink, don't hesitate. Nothing matters except keeping Savannah here, under my protection. "This buys her safety until we figure out the next steps."

The pounding in my head intensifies, matching the throbbing in my ribs. My mouth is blood and the edges of my vision are starting to blur, darkness creeping in like the shadows that always seem to find me.

I really need a drink right now. Something strong enough to dull this fire burning through my side, to quiet the screaming demon in my head.

But this business needs settling first.

The club comes before comfort. Always has.

I plant my feet wider, lock my knees to keep from swaying. The floor seems to tilt beneath me, but I refuse to show weakness.

Not here. Not now. "So. Are we good?"

Brick still doesn't look satisfied. His eyes narrow to winter slits, the kind of cold that kills men who underestimate it. The money I've thrown down—my whole future—isn't enough. I can see it in the way his jaw works, grinding thoughts between his teeth like he's processing something bitter and unpalatable.

"There's more," I say, the words scraping out of me like they're made of barbed wire and desperation. "The Ashbys owe me now."

I feel Diesel shift his weight behind me, leather creaking as his massive frame adjusts. This is new information to him too. I can practically hear the gears turning in his head, calculating what this means for the club.

"Cash and Wyatt know. They know this isn't over. I will…" I sigh. Tired. Hating that I have to make this promise. "I will give up my right to vengeance for the sake of the Club. I will smooth it all over. They're old money. They're used to this kind of bargaining. It's a second language to them. It's a game, ya know? If I want in, they'll play."

Brick's expression doesn't change, but I see the thinking going on behind his eyes—cold, precise arithmetic of power and leverage.

His face might be stone, but his mind is always counting.

"And Marcus White Jr.—the senator's boy—" I add. "He's tranquilized but breathing. He's obviously a psychopath. But his father has a name to protect. You know how boys like that are. In the shadow they rise, in the shadow they fall. Nothin's gonna happen. I'm gonna make sure of it."

The room pulses with my heartbeat, or maybe it's just the blood rushing in my ears. The fluorescent light above us flickers once, casting momentary shadows across Brick's weathered face.

"Hell," I say, ready to sweeten the deal. "Maybe it's a blessin' that those Ashby boys lost their fuckin minds? That I live rent free in their heads? I mean, there's gotta be at least a dozen back-door gun corridors through Ashby land, right?" I've got their full attention now. Kidnapping me isn't enough to put it all on the line. Torturing my woman, not even close.

But securing a new route? One that's not on any map? Yeah. That's somethin' they can get behind. That's worth certain high-risk situations.

I'm not sure I mean it. Even less sure I could actually deliver it.

But I'll say anything right now to keep Savannah

here with me, to build a fortress around her that not even Ashby money can break through.

Brick drums his fingertips against the desk, a slow rhythm that matches the throb in my broken ribs. His eyes never leave mine, searching for weakness, for lies, for the faintest trace of bullshit.

Looking at him, meeting his gaze, takes more strength than I have right now. But he cannot sense weakness or it's over. So I hold as the seconds tick off, one by one, until we're way up in the double digits.

"Level-Two lock down until dawn," he finally says, each word a stone dropped into still water, creating ripples that will change everything. "Havoc, post two extra riflemen at the gate. Anyone approaches, they get one warning shot. Roach, I want our surveillance feeds scrubbed clean—nothing has come in, nothing's gone out in the last seventy-two hours. Ledger—"

Ledger's pen stops its nervous tapping against his notepad.

"Fine him a thousand for seventy-two hours of radio silence." Brick's eyes narrow as they slide up to meet mine. "And for dragging club resources into a personal war." His voice is flat, emotionless, but I can practically hear his thoughts.

He knows exactly what he's taking from me.

A thousand dollars I don't have anymore, not after emptying my pockets on his desk.

Ledger starts scribbling on a piece of paper, then comes at me with a knife. I open my palm, he cuts it, then I place my opposite thumb in the pool of blood and press it to the IOU. "Done," I say. Looking Brick in the eyes as he scoops up my twenty grand. "Now. Are we good?"

Brick holds my gaze as he hands my stash over to Ledger. "You get one night. That's it. I hope she's worth it, Kane." Then he adds, "Dawn church," as he pushes back from his desk. "Full table vote on the Ashby girl's status. Whether she stays or goes. Whether she's yours to protect or just another problem we need to bury."

I finally breathe again, feeling my lungs fill up after having forgotten how to breath.

One night.

It's better than nothing.

CHAPTER 7
SAVANNAH

I sink deeper into this broken-down couch like it's trying to claim me. The springs beneath me groan with every tiny shift of my weight—a confession of age and overuse. This isn't the kind of furniture that gets replaced when it wears out. It's the kind that wears in, collecting stories in its stains.

Legion's clothes hang off me like a child playing dress-up. His shirt smells like him—motor oil, and soap, and something darker underneath. My fingertips brush against a tear in the seam, tracing it like braille. The fabric's worn thin from years of washing.

My mouth is so dry and my tongue isn't working right. Whatever Marcus gave me has left my throat parched as prairie dirt. I'd kill for a water, but I'm not gonna ask. Can't speak. Not here, where every word feels like it might be priced differently than what I'm used to.

The air hangs thick around me—cigarettes, and whiskey, and male sweat. Like breathing through a filter of secrets and testosterone. Smoke drifts in lazy circles beneath the dim lights, never quite finding its way out.

Like me.

A bead of sweat slides down my neck, disappearing into the collar of Legion's shirt. I feel… empty. Like someone scooped out everything inside me that was important and left just enough behind to keep breathing.

Three days tied to that bed with Marcus hovering over me, feeding me drugs, and lies, and cherry pie.

I don't know that I'll get over this. I can't see a way.

And while all these thoughts circle me like the smoke, the clubhouse breathes around me. Men move through doorways on the far side of the room, their boots heavy on the floor. Their eyes slide over me—curious, suspicious, calculating—before moving on.

I'm cargo. Something Legion dragged in bleeding.

A complication.

The lights buzz overhead, not bright enough to chase away the shadows in the corners, just enough to make sure nobody trips over the furniture. Just enough to see the blood dried on my wrists where the zip ties cut in.

I bring my knees up to my chest, hugging myself. Making myself smaller. I feel like I'm in the wolf's den. Sitting here in borrowed clothes, with no shoes, no phone, and no idea what happens next.

The room is loud in a silent way.

Men shuffle cards at a table in the corner, the snap of worn paper against wood the only real sound. Someone coughs. Ice clinks in a glass. A chair scrapes. But it's the quiet that presses in on me—the weight of all the words they aren't saying.

No one talks directly to me, but they're all looking.

Quick glances, sidelong stares, eyes that measure and dismiss in the same breath. A man with a gray beard scratches his neck and mutters something to his neighbor. They both turn to study me like I'm an exotic animal that wandered into their territory. Another leans against the bar, whiskey in hand, watching me over the rim of his glass. His gaze doesn't waver even when I catch him.

Leather cuts, patched vests, scarred knuckles, tattoos that don't mean art—they mean warning.

These are not my people.

They all look hungry.

Not the kind of hunger that gets satisfied with food. It's deeper, older—the hunger of men who've spent their lives taking what they need because nobody ever gave them anything.

These men don't believe in filters or appearances. They've stripped life down to its bones—loyalty, territory, survival. The neon beer signs and tattered pool table are just dressing on something much more primal. It hums in the air like electricity before a storm.

I don't belong here.

Behind the bar stands a glass-fronted case filled with liquor bottles—the good stuff, I'm guessing—secured with a padlock that's hanging half-open. Like they can't decide if they're protecting it from outsiders or each other.

Overhead, a ceiling fan turns with a slow, rhythm. It clacks once every revolution, the sound becoming a metronome to my scattered thoughts. Marking time in a place where minutes disappear.

I shift my attention to the clubhouse walls, desperate for something to focus on besides the men watching me. They're a chaotic collage—photographs, plaques, and club memorabilia stacked like sedimentary layers of history. Everything's coated in a film of dust and neglect, like these memories aren't meant to be polished, just preserved in their original grit.

The photographs draw me in—finally something I understand. Pictures. Documentation. Evidence. My mother's obsession, my childhood prison, my professional language.

These aren't studio portraits with perfect lighting. They're snapshots of club parties, ceremonies, initiations. Men with arms thrown over each other's shoulders, standing before motorcycles or around fires, their eyes dead-serious beneath the brims of caps or bandanas. Not a single smile among them. Not even a hint.

This isn't the kind of family that takes Christmas card photos or gathers for professional portraits at JCPenney. This is the kind that buries its secrets six feet under and drinks until the memories blur around the edges. The kind that measures loyalty in scars and silence.

The images feel loud somehow. Gritty. Greasy. Like a prayer said backward. They don't invite you in—they dare you to look away.

I search the faces, wondering if Legion is in any of these frames. Wondering what stories these walls would tell if they could speak. What confessions they've absorbed from drunken mouths at three in the morning.

I think about the Book of Legion hidden in my safe room—my mother's obsessive documentation of a boy growing into a man. What would a Book of Badlands look like? Would it be bound in leather like my mother's albums, or would it be scattered across these walls, these tables, these scarred bodies?

The difference between my world and this one hits me like a slap. In my photos, everything is staged—the lighting perfect, the pose practiced, the story controlled.

Here, the images are raw. Real.

They don't try to be anything other than what they are.

Moments captured between blood and brotherhood.

I close my eyes and pray to a God I don't think is listening anymore. Not for salvation. Just for this moment to end. For my mind to stop whirling like creek water over stones. For the club walls to stop closing in.

My throat clicks when I swallow. I hug myself. Wrapping my arms around my pulled-up legs and rest my chin on my knees.

I don't feel right. I don't feel like me.

Every sound in this place hits too hard. Pool balls cracking together. Whiskey bottles clinking. Low voices murmuring things I can't quite catch. Men shifting in leather cuts that creak like old saddles. The building itself seems to breathe—exhaling cigarette smoke, inhaling tension.

"Savannah..."

My name floats across the room, a whisper meant to be heard. But I miss the rest. A woman's voice, gruff as sandpaper. I glance up to find the source—a silver-haired woman leaning against the bar, arms crossed over her chest. She's not looking at me now, but I know she was. Everyone is, even when they pretend not to be.

A girl walks by, whisperin' something about my bare feet. I ignore it, turning my face away.

I can still taste cherry pie.

I will never eat cherry pie again. It's a symbol now of everything I want to forget.

I want to brush my teeth until my gums bleed. And even though Legion washed me off before we came here, I feel covered in dust and smoke. I want to scrub every inch of skin with steel wool and bleach.

I want to go home.

I want Legion.

Not just near me, not just in the same room. I want him on me, around me, holding me like a shield between my body and the world. I want his arms locked around me, his chest against my back, his breath in my hair.

I'm drowning in open air and I need his hand.

I don't know how to live in this world of outlaw bikers who all look like killers.

I need Legion, and he's gone, and I'm alone in a room full of men who see me as nothing but trouble.

The door swings open with a rush of air that cuts through the smoke.

Every head turns.

Legion walks through the threshold, his eyes lock onto mine like I'm the only thing in the world. The bruises on his face have darkened since the rescue, purple-black against his skin. There's dried blood at the corner of his mouth he didn't bother to wipe away.

He looks tense.

Whatever happened in that room, it didn't go how he planned. It wasn't victory.

When he comes towards me, the men part around him without a word, making space so he can pass.

When he reaches me, he crouches down in front of the couch. Close enough that I can smell sweat and blood on him, but he doesn't touch me. Doesn't brush my hair back or take my hand like he usually would.

He just meets my eyes, his gaze steady but haunted. "I know you don't understand my world…" He blows out a breath. "I get it. What we do here, what we've built here." He stops to swallow. "It doesn't mean anything to you, Savannah."

He lifts up his shirt, showing me the bandage over his heart. He rips the gauze off, takes my hand, and presses my fingertips to the burned skin. "It's everything to me. It's not more than you, Savannah. I need you to know that. But there is no *you* without this place. I need you to understand that too."

I don't understand. None of this makes sense.

"We only have until dawn," he continues.

My mouth is so dry, I can barely speak. "Only have what until dawn?"

"Protection. They're gonna vote on you. Every patched member will come in tonight at some point and stay until dawn. Then we have church—not the kind you go to—and they will vote. Should Badlands shoulder responsibility for the Little Ashby Princess?"

I blink. Unable to believe he just called me that.

"Or should we cut her loose?"

I swallow again—my god, I need some fucking water. "Maybe I should just go? If I'm causing all this trouble."

"Well," Legion says. And now is when he touches me. Puts his hands on my knees. "We've got a problem there too, darlin'. Because I *live* here. Yeah, I have the new trailer, but this is home. And if you leave now, I can't come with you."

I scoff. Is he fuckin' serious right now? He can't come with me.

"It's not how it sounds," Legion continues.

"Oh, I think it is, Legion. I think it's exactly how it sounds."

"I'm not telling you to go, I'm not telling you to stay." He leans in closer, whispering now. "I'm telling you that if I walk out, they're gonna kill me."

"What?" No sound comes out of my mouth when I ask this.

"The brand, Savannah, it's a promise for life. And when I made this promise two weeks ago, I thought you were safe. I thought we'd stay in our places and live our lives, and... " He throws up his hands. "Whatever. Hook up, maybe. Or never see each other again. I don't know. But that's not how I feel tonight. Tonight, you're mine. And I want it to stay that way."

"I don't understand. Why would they kill you if I left?"

"Because I'd go with you. And, like I said, I can't go with you."

It takes a moment for all this cryptic shit to fall into place, but eventually, it does.

If you leave, I can't go.

But if I leave, he's going with me.

It what I wanted, wasn't it? That's what I told him the very day they took us. If I walk away, he walks too.

He said no. He made it very clear that he was not walkin' out on Badlands.

Now I know why. It's not because he doesn't love me.

It's because of that stupid brand.

They own him.

That's what that brand means.

And if I get up and walk out of here tonight, he's going with me.

Will they kill him in front of me? Immediately? Kill us both?

Or will they let us walk away and hunt us down later?

I take a breath, hold it, and slowly let it out. "OK. So... what do you want me to do, Legion?" Because clearly, he needs me to do something.

My suspicion is confirmed when he smiles. "That's the spirit. And it's not even a big ask. Just... " He pauses. Like he knows he's lying. Whatever he's about to say, it's a huge ask, but he wants to convince me it's not. "Ya just... make them like ya, baby." He leans forward and kisses me. His hand wrapping around my head, fisting my hair.

And it's so nice, this kiss. This touching. It's so much of what I need, that I kiss him back. Grabbing his head now too.

I hear the laughing. The remarks—the approval—all around us.

"See," Legion says. "That's all you got to do. Make them like you by loving me. By accepting my protection. By being *mine*."

I don't quite understand what this means. My confusion must spread across my face because Legion sits down next to me and pulls me into his lap, making me straddle his legs.

I don't like turning my back on the room, but Legion's got my face in his hands now, so I can't look back. He stares up at me, eyes pleading for my understanding. Nearly begging.

"What?" I whisper. "What aren't you saying?"

"We're gonna fuck, Savannah."

"What?" I try and look behind me, but Legion holds my face in place.

"You heard me. I'm gonna fuck you on this couch and mark you as mine. Everyone's gonna watch and get the hint. You are one of *us* now. You are choosing me, and by choosing me, you choose them."

"Choose *them*?"

Legion must see the panic in my face because he shakes his head. "Not like that. You *are* mine. And if you fuck me here, they'll know it. Because if you're mine you will do everything I say, even this. In front of them."

"This is what they want?" I scoff again. "Voyeur sex?"

"It's your surrender, Savannah. That's what they want. To know who's side you're on. Mine? Ours? Badlands?" He narrows his eyes at me. It turns him into someone I don't know. "Or the Ashby's."

"You, the man who saved me? Or them, the ones

who hate me?" I let out a breath and place my hands on his face now. "It's not even a choice. It's you. It's always been you."

This does not make him smile. Instead, his face grows harder. "You have to own it, or none of this is gonna work."

Very complicated things are happening in this clubhouse that I do not understand. Whatever went on in that back room he just came out of, didn't quite land the way he hoped.

He wants me to prove something here.

Prove to these men that I am... owned.

Controlled.

Oh. I nearly laugh, that's how suddenly the understanding floods into me.

Fucking me here on this couch, in front of everyone, is a claim. But more than that, it's... a pecking order.

Men. *Then* women.

Right.

Well, I came up in a matriarchy. My mother ran our family the same way she ran our ranch. It was a business. She used me like a product. Turned me into content. Took everything from me.

What more could these men take?

My soul was sold long before I rode into this compound on the back of a bike.

Legion is asking me to submit to him under the watchful gaze of his biker brothers. To convince them I am his. I will obey. I will not be a threat, or a liability, or a weakness.

I will be a good girl who does as she's told.

I will fit in.

Fine. If this is the cost, it's a price I can pay.

I reach down, grab the hem of my t-shirt and hoodie, and I pull them up over my head.

No bra, tits right in his face.

The approvals all around me are immediate.

Legion's smile, and his relief, also happen instantaneously. He looks me in the eyes and says, "This is just part one, just so you know. The sex, it's just part one."

CHAPTER 8
LEGION

I keep my voice low, meant only for her, but I know every fucking man in this room is straining to hear. "You ready to show them who you belong to?"

Savannah's eyes hold mine, blue as high-country sky, wide but not afraid. Not anymore. There's something else there now—determination. Spite, maybe. The kind that carries you through disappointment.

She stands up from my lap, slow and deliberate, like she's got all night and we're the only two people in the room. Every head is turned this way. All eyes on her bare back, on the curve where her spine disappears into my jeans riding low on her hips. But she doesn't acknowledge them. Not once.

Her focus is a physical thing, like hands on my skin. She doesn't look away from my face as she kneels down in front of me and reaches for my belt. Her fingers work the buckle with practiced ease.

"Lift," she whispers, and I raise my hips so she can tug my jeans down.

My cock falls out. It lies along my thigh, hard and thick.

She licks her lips, then whispers, "Beautiful," like we're alone.

Somewhere behind her, Diesel coughs. Chains mutters something I can't make out. I don't give a fuck. Not when Savannah's hands are sliding up my thighs.

She tugs at my jacket, and I lean forward so she can pull it off and down my arms. The cut comes off next. Then my shirt follows, up and over my head.

Now we're even. Both half-naked in a room full of fully-dressed men. Both vulnerable. Both choosing this.

Her hand wraps around my cock, and I hiss through my teeth at the contact. Her palm is soft, her grip firm as she strokes me, base to tip, slow and measured.

"That's it," I murmur, just for her. "Show me what that hand can do."

She works me steadily, her rhythm perfect, her eyes never leaving mine. I slide down in the cushions a little more, giving her better access, spreading my legs wider.

"Fuck, Savannah," I breathe, as her thumb circles the head, spreading the wetness there. "Yeah, baby. Just like that."

The room around us fades. The men, the smoke, the worn-out couch beneath me—it all disappears until there's nothing but her grip on my shaft and her eyes locked with mine.

Savannah licks her lips and I nod. "Yes," I say, giving her permission. "You can suck me off now, baby. Take my cock in your mouth."

She leans down, and the first touch of her mouth against my cock is pure bliss. Warm and wet. Her lips part to take me in and I can't stop the groan that escapes. My hands find her hair, tangling in the soft strands, not to guide, but to anchor myself. To remind myself this is real.

"Christ, you're perfect," I tell her as she takes me deeper, her tongue flat against the underside. "Look at you, you perfect fuckin' angel. Taking my cock so good. Like you mean it."

She hums around me, the vibration shooting straight up my spine. Her eyes are on mine, pupils blown wide, as she works me with her mouth.

"That's it, baby," I encourage, my voice rougher now. "Fuck, you're so beautiful with your lips stretched around me."

She hollows her cheeks, sucking harder, and I tighten my grip in her hair.

"You like that?" I ask, knowing she does. "You like the taste of me?"

She nods slightly, never breaking rhythm, never looking away.

"Tell me," I demand, needing to hear it. Needing everyone to hear it.

She pulls off with an obscene pop, her lips wet and swollen. "I love it," she says, loud enough for the room to hear. "I love the way you taste. The way you feel in my mouth."

Then she's back on me, taking me deeper this time, until I feel the back of her throat.

"Fuck," I groan, lifting my hips up, pushing myself

deeper. Unable to hold back. "Just like that, Savannah. Take it all."

Her hand works what her mouth can't, twisting slightly on the upstroke in a way that makes my thighs tense. Every time the tip of my head hits the top of her mouth, I grit my teeth. My breathing gets heavier, more ragged as she finds a rhythm that's pushing me toward the edge faster than I want.

I'm dimly aware of the room around us—the shuffling of feet, the clink of bottles, the heavy silence of men watching something sacred and profane all at once. But none of it matters. Nothing matters but the woman kneeling before me, claiming me as thoroughly as I'm claiming her.

"Eyes on me," I remind her when her gaze starts to drift. "Look at me while you suck me off."

She obeys instantly, her eyes locking back on mine. There's a flush spreading across her chest now, up her neck to her cheeks. She's getting turned on by this—by pleasuring me, by being watched, by the power she has even on her knees.

"That's my girl," I praise, voice tight with restraint. "Taking me so deep. Making me feel so good."

Her rhythm speeds up, her hand and mouth working in perfect tandem. She moans around me, the sound vibrating through my cock, and I know she's getting wet. Know she's aching for me to touch her too.

Soon. But not yet.

"You gonna make me come?" I ask, my voice barely more than a growl. "You want my come down your throat, baby? Want everyone to see what you do to me?"

She nods, eyes never leaving mine, and takes me deeper still.

My hand tightens in her hair, holding her steady as my hips start to move, small thrusts I can't control.

"Fuck, Savannah," I groan. "Nobody's ever made me feel like you do. Nobody."

And it's true. No one else has ever stripped me bare like this—not just my body, but something deeper. Something I thought was buried too far down to reach.

She's found it though. Found me. And now she's showing everyone that I'm hers as much as she's mine.

Her tongue swirls around the head of my cock on the upstroke, and I feel the tension building at the base of my spine. Not yet. Not fucking yet.

"Slow down," I command, tugging gently on her hair. "I'm not done with you."

She eases back, her pace becoming torturous, deliberate. Each stroke of her tongue, each hollowing of her cheeks, each press of her lips is measured now. Designed to keep me right on the edge without pushing me over.

"That's it," I encourage. "Nice and slow. Show me how much you want it."

Her eyes never leave mine, and in them, I see everything—desire, determination, a hint of defiance. But most of all, I see choice. She's choosing this.

Choosing me.

Choosing *us*.

And fuck if that isn't the hottest thing I've ever seen.

"Stop," I command, my voice rough with need.

She pulls off immediately, lips slick, eyes questioning.

"Take your pants off."

Savannah stands without hesitation, thumbs hooking into the waistband of my borrowed jeans. They slide down her thighs, pooling at her feet. She steps out of them, standing before me in nothing but her own skin.

The bruises on her thighs are purple shadows, and I swallow hard at the sight of them, anger and desire warring inside me.

I pat my lap, cock still hard and wet from her mouth. "Come here."

She climbs onto me, straddling my thighs, her hand wrapping around my length again. Her touch is confident, sure, like she's handled me a thousand times. And she has—but never like this, never with eyes on us.

I grab her breasts. They're perfect—full and heavy in my palms as I cup them, thumbs brushing over her nipples until they harden.

"You're so fucking beautiful," I murmur, leaning forward to take one nipple into my mouth.

"Oh god," she gasps, her head falling back, arching as I suck hard, then gentle, then hard again.

Her hand keeps working me, steady and relentless. I switch to her other breast, giving it the same attention, feeling her thighs tense around mine.

I glance up, taking in the room without breaking rhythm. The bar's gone quiet except for the occasional clink of glass and low murmurs. Every eye is on us—on Savannah's back as it arches, on my mouth at her breast, on her hand stroking my cock.

Some of the guys have their women now, pulling them onto laps, hands wandering under shirts. Diesel nods at me from across the room, approval in his eyes. Brick stands near the door, arms crossed, expression unreadable as always.

The door swings open, and more men file in—patched members and pledges alike, heeding the call to come vote in church tomorrow. Others who'd been out on runs. They stop short, taking in the scene, then move to the bar for drinks, eyes never leaving us.

Every patched member will be here soon. Every one of them will see Savannah choose me—choose us—over everything she's ever known.

It burns that it has to be this way, that she has to prove herself like this. But I'm relieved too, because I think we'll win the vote.

I think they'll let her stay.

I refocus on Savannah, on the woman I've loved since I was too young to understand what love even meant. There's never been a day since that first time at the silo when I didn't tell her I loved her at least once in my head.

In prison, her name was a prayer I whispered into my pillow.

A promise I made to myself every morning when I woke up in that concrete box.

Now, with her here, as part of the club, she'll be mine for real. Nothing will ever come between us again. No family, no money, no bars, no time.

"Lift up," I tell her, voice low and urgent.

She rises on her knees, understanding immediately. I position myself at her entrance. She's wet—so fucking wet—and the knowledge that this turns her on as much as it does me makes my cock throb.

"Sit down on my cock, baby," I whisper against her ear. "Show everyone who you belong to."

She sinks down slowly, taking me inch by inch, her breath hitching as I fill her. When she's fully seated, I cup her face, thumb brushing over her cheekbone.

"You feel that?" I ask, voice raw. "Feel how perfect we fit together? Like you were made for me."

"Yes," she breathes, eyes locked on mine. "Only you, Legion. It's only ever been you."

I smooth sweaty strands of hair from her face, tucking them behind her ear. My hand lingers on her cheek, a tender gesture at odds with the filthy words spilling from my lips.

"Your pussy's so tight around me, so fucking wet. You like them watching us? Like them seeing how good you take my cock?"

She nods, a moan escaping her as I thrust up slightly.

"Say it," I demand. "Tell me what you want."

"I want you to fuck me," she says, loud enough for everyone to hear. "I want them to see that I'm yours. Only yours."

That's all I need to hear. I wrap my arms around her waist and start moving in earnest, driving up into her as she grinds down on me. The couch creaks beneath us, the sound almost lost under Savannah's moans.

"That's it, baby," I encourage, voice tight with restraint. "Take what you need. Show them how good I make you feel."

She rides me hard, her nails digging into my shoulders, her breasts bouncing with each thrust. I grip her hips, guiding her, setting a rhythm that has us both panting.

"Fuck, Legion," she gasps, head thrown back. "Just like that. Don't stop."

I have no intention of stopping. Not when she feels this good, this right. Not when every thrust brings me closer to something I've been chasing for more than a decade.

"You gonna come for me?" I ask, voice rough. "Gonna come on my cock with everyone watching?"

"Yes," she moans, movements becoming more frantic. "I'm close. So close."

I slide one hand between us, finding her clit with my thumb. She jerks at the contact, a sharp cry escaping her.

"That's it," I urge. "Let go, Savannah. Let them hear you."

She shatters around me, walls clenching tight as she comes with a wail that echoes through the room. Her body trembles, her nails drawing blood as she clings to me.

The sight of her coming undone pushes me over the edge. I thrust up hard one last time, burying myself deep as I come, her name a broken sound on my lips.

For a moment, we're frozen like that—connected, breathless, trembling. Then she collapses against me, face buried in my neck, and I wrap my arms around her, holding her close.

Around us, the room shifts back to life.

Conversations resume, pool balls crack against each other, women laugh as they settle onto their men's laps.

It's like someone turned the volume back up on a scene that had been muted.

We sit there on the couch, sweaty and satisfied, still joined.

I stroke her back, feeling her heartbeat gradually slow against my chest.

She fits against me perfectly, like she always has.

CHAPTER 9
SAVANNAH

I rest my cheek against Legion's shoulder, eyelids heavy. My body's gone liquid, muscles turned to warm honey as I melt against him. The room blurs at the edges. Drugs still haunting my blood, making everything feel like it's happening underwater.

I could sleep right here, right now. Skin against skin, his heartbeat under my palm. I don't care who watches.

Legion's hand slides down my back, cups my ass with a firm squeeze that jolts me halfway to consciousness.

"We're not done yet, princess," he murmurs, lips brushing my ear. "That was a good first step. Probably got half the members on your side, but the night is young. And that means—"

"For fuck's sake!" A voice thunders through the bar, sharp as a gunshot. "Are we at a goddamn wake or what?"

I jerk upright, arms instinctively crossing over my chest despite what everyone's already seen. A mountain of a man stands at the back of the room—wide-framed with wild eyes and an open shirt revealing a torso that's more ink than skin. He stares directly at me, beckoning with one massive hand.

"Hey, Diesel, shut your hole," someone calls from a corner table.

Diesel. The one who's been watching Mercy. The one who taught her to shoot.

He throws both arms up like he's conducting an orchestra, and the entire place goes silent. Even the ceiling fan seems to pause. He steps into that silence like it belongs to him, crossing the room in three long strides before slamming his palm on the bar hard enough to make bottles jump.

"Feels like a damn funeral in here," he announces, voice filling every corner. "Someone better pour this girl a drink before her nerves chew through the fucking cushion." He looks at me, eyes narrowed but mouth quirked up. "Time to welcome the girl who broke the bad boy's brain, don't you think?"

The scene shifts faster than I can track. Music erupts from hidden speakers—something with a growl and a bass line that crawls up my spine. I flinch at the sudden assault, curling closer to Legion. The men at the corner table laugh, the sound rough like gravel. Someone cranks the volume until I feel it in my teeth.

The room transforms like a beast waking.

Like the blood came back.

"Come on, pretty girl," Diesel yells, gesturing toward the bar. The way he says it sounds like an invitation wrapped in barbed wire.

Legion's hand finds my knee, squeezes once. "Go

with it," he says quietly. "Try. Breathe." His eyes search mine, desperate for understanding. "This is our only chance, Savannah. This night is it. Once the vote is done, it's over. It's law. And if they don't let you stay—"

He doesn't finish. But he doesn't have to. It's already been said.

"Come on," Legion says, cupping my face.

"Pretty Girl!" another man calls. "We're all waitin' on ya!"

"It's not that bad," Legion says. "I promise. They're good people."

I don't even respond with words, just a look. Which makes Legion laugh. "I get it," he says. "I know what you see. But that's because you're not family yet. If we get the votes, you will be. And then you'll see. Then you'll understand. These men will protect you 'till the end of time. You'll never know how you got along without them."

And that's that. His speech is over because he doesn't even give me a chance to respond. He just gently pushes me off his lap, stands up, tucks his cock back into his jeans, and zips up like nothing happened.

Then he shoulders into his cut, the leather settling across his back like armor, and walks toward the bar without looking back.

I sit alone on the couch, naked.

The gaze of forty or fifty outlaw bikers tracking my every breath.

I stare at Legion's back as he walks away. I'm supposed to follow. I understand that much. But what waits for me at that bar, where the men gather with hungry eyes?

I have no idea.

Something inside me wants to say no. To curl up right here on this stained couch and refuse.

But if I do, we lose everything.

I won't be protected.

Won't be allowed to stay.

And Legion won't be allowed to leave.

The rational part of my brain understands they're not just gonna kick me through the gate and tell me to walk home. We're in the middle of absolute nowhere. I don't even know where the nearest town is. Hell, I don't even know where I am right now.

Legion wouldn't abandon me. He'd get me somewhere safe.

But then he'd leave. And I'd be alone.

I'd be fine, obviously. One phone call to my lawyer would get me money, clothes, a car—anything I needed. Eleanor Ashby's daughter is never truly stranded.

But I cannot go home. Not after what they did.

Legion is my home now.

I stand up slowly, deliberately, letting the room watch me gather myself. I pull on his t-shirt, slide into his jeans, zip up his hoodie. Like it never happened. Like I wasn't just naked beneath the gaze of fifty strangers.

My mother taught me how to smile through anything, and this is just one more performance.

I walk toward the bar, chin up, shoulders back. Every step feels like a mile. My bare feet stick to the floor—beer spills and God knows what else making each footfall a tacky reminder of how far I've fallen. The conversations around me dip and swell like prairie grass in wind.

"Rich girls slummin' it," someone mutters from a dark corner.

Another voice says something I don't catch—something that makes three men laugh low and mean.

I keep walking anyway.

The music kicks harder, some growling anthem about women and whiskey. The crowd shifts around me, bodies rearranging like I'm a stone dropped in still water. A few people lean in, curious, waiting to see what happens next.

I reach the bar where Legion stands with Diesel. Legion positions himself beside me, close enough that his body heat reaches through the borrowed clothes. He doesn't touch me. Doesn't speak. But his presence steadies me like a hand on a spooked horse's flank.

The night has started. Whatever happens next will decide if I get to stay or if I have to run. I grip the edge of the bar, feel the sticky wood under my fingertips. I breathe in through my nose. Hold it.

Make them like me? This has to be a joke.

These men don't want to like me. They want to own a piece of me, same as everyone else. Same as my mother with her camera. Same as Marcus with his ring. Same as Cash with his threats about inheritance.

But I'm still here.

Still standing.

And I've been making men like me since before I even knew what that meant. What's forty or fifty more?

Diesel's gaze cuts through me from behind the bar. Not a smile or a nod. Just that stare, assessing me like

I'm a filly at auction. The glass he slides toward me is chipped along the rim, a jagged imperfection that might slice my lip if I'm not careful. The whiskey inside catches light from the neon beer signs, turning gold, then amber, then something darker as it sloshes against the sides. It reminds me of sunset through my bedroom window at home—a place that isn't mine anymore.

I lift the shot, feel its weight. Everyone's watching, waiting to see if Eleanor Ashby's perfect daughter will choke, or cry, or run.

I tip it back in one smooth motion.

The burn traces a map down my throat. The alcohol illuminates my injuries from the inside out, making me glow with hurt.

Before the sting fades from my tongue, Diesel places a second shot in front of me. No words. Just expectation.

I don't hesitate this time. Down it goes, chasing the first, pooling like liquid courage in my empty stomach. The drugs still lingering in my system dance with the whiskey, making my fingertips tingle and my cheeks flush.

A third glass appears. I can feel Legion watching me, his presence a gravity well I'm circling. I wonder if he's proud, or worried, or both.

I down the third shot, no longer tasting it.

The fourth glass arrives with a slight nod from Diesel, the barest acknowledgment that I'm exceeding expectations. The whiskey no longer burns—it warms, spreading through limbs that have been cold since Cash dragged me away from Legion at the silo.

And finally… it fades.

All of it.

it just fades and... it feels good.

Legion leans in as the men get rowdy. I think maybe they might like me. I think maybe I did OK.

And as these words form in my head, my mouth does something weird.

It smiles.

Not the smile my mother taught me—perfect teeth, practiced dimples, eyes that crinkle just enough to seem genuine on camera.

This smile is wilder, looser at the edges.

It belongs to the girl who used to meet Legion in secret, who gave herself to him under stars and grain dust while a dynasty waited at home.

This smile says: I'm not done yet.

This isn't over yet.

I'm here.

The whiskey settles into my bones, making everything soft at the edges. The room doesn't spin exactly, but it feels like I'm watching it through water. Colors blur. Sounds stretch. I lean against the bar, feeling the press of Legion's body beside me.

Across from us, Diesel laughs at something Legion says. I don't catch the words, just the low rumble of Legion's voice and the answering bark from Diesel. Their camaraderie feels strange—intimate in a way I've never understood.

Brotherhood, maybe.

Whatever it is, it makes Legion's face relax. The hard lines around his mouth soften.

He looks... happy.

And that—that single moment of seeing joy crack

through his mask—makes something in my chest uncoil. If he can be happy here, with these men, maybe I can too. Maybe this isn't just survival. Maybe it's something else.

The music changes, shifting from something angry and pounding to a slower beat that feels like honey in my veins. I sway slightly, letting the rhythm catch me.

That's when I notice him.

A man materializes beside Legion like he's been summoned from smoke. Older than the others, with a face weathered into permanent vigilance. His leather cut is different—heavier with patches, worn like a second skin rather than a uniform. The patch at the top reads "President" in faded stitching. Below it, "Brick."

The man who holds Legion's loyalty.

He's speaking to Legion, but his eyes are fixed on me. Not examining my body like the others. Not assessing my worth or my use. He's looking at *me*, like he's trying to read what's written under my skin.

"What do we call her?" Brick asks Legion, his voice cutting through the murmur of conversation.

The room goes silent.

Everyone is watching us. Waiting. I realize with sudden clarity that this is some kind of test or ritual. My name—my real name—doesn't matter here. What matters is what Legion claims me as.

Legion doesn't hesitate. Doesn't even blink.

"Mine," he says, pointing to his chest. Simple. Direct. Like it's the only answer that could ever exist. "You will all call her *Mine*."

The word drops between us, heavy with meaning. Not a question. Not a request. A statement of fact.

Brick's weathered face remains impassive for a heartbeat. Two. Then something like approval flickers across his features. He lifts his pint glass, the amber liquid catching light as he raises it high.

"Everyone say hello to 'Not Mine'!" he announces to the room, his voice carrying authority without volume.

A chorus of rough voices echoes back: "Hello, Not Mine!"

I feel my face crack into another smile—looser than before, whiskey-warm and genuine. This is absurd. This whole night is absurd. I should be terrified or outraged. Instead, I'm floating somewhere between fear and fascination, watching myself become something new.

Legion's hand slides down my back, settling possessively on my ass. He squeezes once, firm enough to claim but gentle over the bruises I know are forming there. He leans in close, his lips brushing against the sensitive skin below my ear.

"Mine," he whispers, just for me.

The word shivers through me like a current. I take a deep breath, feeling my chest expand against his borrowed shirt, and nod.

Yes. His. At least for tonight, I am only this: the thing Legion wants bad enough to fight for.

"Hey, Demon." A man slides up beside me, bumping my shoulder.

I blink at him, trying to focus. His cut says *Chains*. He's holding a black Sharpie between tattooed fingers, tapping it against Legion's head like a schoolyard taunt.

"Want me to mark her for you?" he asks, waggling the marker.

I open my mouth to say something—what, I don't

know—but I'm distracted by his eye. One is normal, dark brown. The other is a vivid, unnatural red, like something from a horror film. It catches the light weirdly, too glossy. I stare at it, forgetting everything my mama taught me about polite society.

That eye can't be real. It's glass, or plastic, or something else entirely. But it *moves* with the other one, tracking back and forth. I can't look away from it.

I'm so fixated on the man's freakish eye that I don't register what's happening until Legion's fingers curl under the hem of my borrowed t-shirt. He lifts the fabric, exposing my tits.

"Just go with it," Legion murmurs in my ear, his breath warm against my skin.

A laugh bubbles up from my chest—not my camera laugh, not my charity function laugh—but something genuine and slightly hysterical. I'm standing in an outlaw biker clubhouse with my tits exposed while a one-eyed man uncaps a Sharpie with his teeth.

The marker is cold against my skin. Inciting chills that quickly pull my breasts up, making my nipples tighten. Chains works with surprising delicacy, the tip of the Sharpie tracing over the curves of my body with skill.

The chemical smell rises, sharp and familiar. I don't resist. I stand still, feeling the slight tickle as Chains moves the marker with unexpected precision. He's looking at me with both eyes now—the normal one and the red one—and there's something like respect in his gaze.

"There," he says, stepping back to admire his handiwork.

I look down. Across my tits, in thick black letters that curve with my body, he's written: *PROPERTY OF DEMON*.

And the letters are nice too. Tattoo letters, I realize. Not handwriting. This man, covered in ink, must be the one who does all the drawing.

I am not a tattoo girl, but I like this claim.

I want everyone to see it so I turn and face the club. All eyes on me, again. And I yell it. Loud and clear.

"Property of Demon!"

When I find Legions face again, his eyes are smilin'. And it might be the most real smile I've ever seen on him. They move from the words on my skin to my face, and I see what he's not saying.

I did it. I made them like me.

No, that's not quite right. I made them accept me as *his*.

As Legion's.

As belonging to the man they call Demon.

The room shifts around us, the energy changing. Men nod at Legion as they pass, lifting their drinks in silent acknowledgment. A few slap his shoulder or bump fists with him. Someone whistles, and another voice calls out something crude that makes Legion's jaw tighten briefly before relaxing again.

I lean against him, drunk, and drugged, and happy. Feeling the solid wall of his chest behind me. His arms wrap around my waist, holding me steady. His fingers trace the edge of the letters on my skin, following Chains' work.

Then he pulls the shirt back down, hiding his claim. Because everyone knows who I am now.

His.

"How's it feel?" Legion whispers, his lips against my ear.

I don't know how to answer. How does it feel to be branded as someone's property? How does it feel to have thrown away everything I was raised to be, everything my mother built, for this man and this moment?

It feels like freedom.

It feels like falling.

It feels like the first honest thing I've done in years.

CHAPTER 10
LEGION

The club settles into a rhythm I recognize—the slow dance of drunk men who've run out of stories to tell but aren't ready to sleep. It's after 3 AM, and I'm countin' minutes. Dawn vote means first light, and in Montana summer, that's comin' by 5.

Savannah leans against me, swaying to some sad country song Butch put on the jukebox. Her eyes keep closing, then snapping open like she's afraid she might miss somethin'.

"You're falling asleep standing up," I tell her, my hand at the small of her back.

"M'not," she mumbles, but her head drops against my chest.

I look around the room. Most of the patched members have filtered in over the last few hours. Roach is at the bar arguing with Ledger over something to do with supply lines. Havoc plays cards with Butch and two prospects in the corner. Diesel's passed out on the leather couch, his feet still planted on the floor. Chains is drawing on the arm of some hangaround who's too drunk to notice.

Brick sits alone at a table near the door, nursing the same whiskey he's had for two hours. Watching. Always watching.

I don't trust leaving the room. Not with the vote comin'. But Savannah's dead on her feet, and I need her rested before whatever comes next.

"Let's get you upstairs," I say, pulling her closer as we sway. Not because I like dancing—I fucking hate it—but because she needs the support to stay upright.

"We should stay," she says, but there's no fight in it. "What if they vote while we're gone?"

"Church isn't till dawn. Women don't get a vote anyway. You won't have anything to do with this vote." I rest my chin on top of her head. "You need sleep."

She doesn't argue. Just nods against my chest, her fingers curled into my cut.

I guide her toward the stairs, one arm around her waist. A few heads turn to watch us go, but no one says anything. That's good. Silence means acceptance—or at least tolerance.

The bunkhouse is down a narrow hallway above the main floor. Ten rooms, most empty tonight since everyone's downstairs waitin' for church. I take her to my room, lead her inside, then close and lock the door behind us. Not that it would stop anyone who really wanted in, but it's a sign.

Savannah stands in the middle of the room, swayin' slightly. I strip off the borrowed clothes—my clothes—and take a moment to admire Chains' work across her tits.

PROPERTY OF DEMON. The letters are perfect, flowing with the curve of her body. Not just scrawled words, but art. He's got that tattoo style down, even with a Sharpie.

Demon. My club name sits strange in my mouth, even now. When a man is named Legion at birth and joins an outlaw club, you'd think it would be enough. But everyone gets a name to keep up the pretenses that the world still offers privacy.

Savannah got named tonight too. *Not Mine*. Brick's way of marking her as off-limits to everyone but me. She knows what it means.

She didn't speak to a single person tonight other than me. Didn't try to charm her way in. She just let me claim her, claimed me back, and somehow that was enough.

I'm pretty sure the vote will go our way.

Pretty sure. But nothing's guaranteed in club life.

I lead her to the small bathroom attached to the room. I feel like that shower we took at the trailer wasn't enough. Especially after a long night standing in smoke and whiskey fumes. This shower's barely big enough for one, but we make it work. Hot water hits us both, washing away a little bit more of the evil we just went through.

Savannah wakes up a little under the spray, blinkin' up at me through wet lashes.

She looks down at her chest, at the letters that will not wash off—not today, at least. "I like it," she says. Smiling as her hand slips between my legs, finding me already half-hard just from having her naked and wet against me.

Her fingers curl around my cock, stroking slow and deliberate.

"Again?" I ask, surprised she's got the energy.

"Again," she confirms, her thumb circling the head.

I lean back against the tiled wall, letting her work me as she kisses her way down my chest and ends up on her knees.

Savannah has had my cock in her mouth many times over the years. But never like tonight. We've actually never spent this much time together. Not all at once.

I fist her hair, moving my hips forward a little so I can feel the muscles of her throat tighten around me, mimicking the way her pussy does it, as I think about earlier.

Her on her knees in front of me, with the whole club watching as she took me in her mouth.

Her on my lap, riding me slow and deep, her submission invading the silence as she rode me, telling them all who she belongs to.

As far as claimings go, I figure mine went pretty perfect.

One day, hopefully today, I'll get a chance to ask her about how she felt about that. What she liked about it, what she didn't. What she might want to do again.

I slip my cock out of Savannah's mouth, her lips making a soft pop. She looks up at me with a hunger I've never seen before.

Good. Let her starve for me. Let me fill her up.

I grab her arm, gentle but firm, and help her to her feet. Her skin is slick under my palm, water beading down the curves of her body. I turn her around, pressin' her front against the tile wall. The water hits my back now, running hot down my spine, steam rising around us.

I lean in, my chest against her back, and kiss the nape of her neck. She shivers. My cock slides between her ass cheeks, not entering her yet, just letting her feel what's coming.

"Spread your legs open for me," I whisper into her mouth as I turn her head to kiss her.

She does, moaning a little into my kiss. As her legs part, I grab her hips and pull her towards me, forcing her to bend a little at the waist and press her hands and cheek against the tiled wall.

I reach down between us, slide a finger against the entrance of her pussy, and find her already wet. And not just from the shower. My fingertips slide around her folds, circling her clit once, twice, before pushing inside her. She gasps, her eyes closed, mouth open in a moan.

"That's it," I murmur, working my fingers in and out of her. "Get nice and ready for me."

She pushes back against my hand, wanting more. I've always loved that about her—how fuckin' greedy she gets when we're alone. How she'll beg without words, just the movement of her body telling me everything I need to know.

I withdraw my fingers and position my cock at her entrance. With one slow thrust, I push inside her, feeling her stretch around me. We both groan. I pause once I'm fully seated, letting her adjust to the fullness.

"You feel so fuckin' good," I tell her, my voice rough against her ear. "So tight around me."

"Legion," she breathes, her forehead pressed against the tile. "Please."

I start to move, slow at first, then pick up the pace. My hands grip her hips, fingers digging into her flesh hard enough to leave marks. Good. I want her marked. Want her to look in the mirror tomorrow and see evidence of me on her body—the Sharpie across her tits, the bruises on her hips, the beard burn between her thighs.

The shower keeps runnin', hot water cascading down our bodies as I fuck her from behind. The sound of skin slapping against skin echoes in the small space, mixing with our heavy breathing and Savannah's little whimpers every time I hit that spot deep inside her.

"Touch yourself," I command, one hand sliding up to grip her throat lightly. "Make yourself come on my cock."

She reaches down between her legs, her fingers finding her clit as I continue to thrust into her. I can feel her getting tighter around me as she works herself.

"That's it, baby," I encourage, my lips against her ear. "Show me how much you want it."

Her breathing gets faster, her movements more desperate. The hand on her throat applies pressure. Just a little. Just a bit. Not enough to hurt, just enough to remind her who's in control.

"You gonna come for me?" I ask, my pace relentless now. "Gonna come all over my cock like a good girl?"

"Yes," she gasps, her body tensing. "Yes, Legion, please—"

"Do it," I growl. "Come for me. Now."

She shatters, her pussy clenching around me in

waves as she cries out my name. I keep fucking her through it, drawing out her pleasure until she's trembling and gasping for breath.

Only then do I allow myself to chase my own release, my thrusts becoming harder, more erratic. The pressure builds at the base of my spine, heat coiling tight in my gut.

"Where do you want it?" I manage to ask, my voice strained with the effort of holding back.

"Inside," she says without hesitation. "I want to feel you."

That's all it takes. I bury myself deep and let go, groaning as I fill her with my release. My forehead drops to her shoulder, teeth sinking into her flesh as I pulse inside her, my breathing ragged.

For a moment, we stay like that, connected, the water washing over us. I'm still inside her, softening now but not wanting to break the connection. My arms wrap around her waist, holdin' her against me.

This is mine.

She is mine.

And I'll kill anyone who tries to take her from me again.

I finally slip out of her, turning her around to face me. Water streams down her face, washing away the exhaustion and fear that's been there since I found her tied to that bed. For a moment, she looks like the girl I used to meet at the silo—young and wild and full of life.

I kiss her, softer now, tasting whiskey and somethin' uniquely her on her tongue. When I pull back, her eyes are heavy-lidded, barely staying open.

"Let's clean you up and get you to bed," I murmur, reaching behind her for the soap. Then I lather her body up. I clean Savannah Ashby like it's a religious experience.

Then I wrap her in a towel and lead her to my bed. She curls up next to me, both of us still wet, still naked. And immediately falls asleep.

But I don't.

I lie next to Savannah, watching her chest rise and fall. The drugs Marcus pumped into her are still workin' their way out, making her sleep heavy like death. Every few breaths, I touch my fingers to her neck, just to be sure. Just to feel that pulse.

I brush hair from her face, careful not to wake her. Sleep's the only peace she's likely to get for a while. No matter how this vote goes, when she wakes up, everything changes for both of us.

I press my lips to her cheek, soft as I can manage. She doesn't stir. Doesn't even twitch.

Then I slide from the bed and dress in silence. Jeans. Boots. T-shirt. My cut goes on last. Sliding it over my shoulders as I look down on my sleeping woman. She's curled on her side now, hand tucked under her cheek like a child. The blanket's slipped down, showing the black marker across her tits. PROPERTY OF DEMON.

If the vote goes wrong, it won't mean much.

I leave, pulling the door closed behind me, and take the stairs slow, each step pulling at the knife-edge pain in my ribs. With all the attention on Savannah, not to mention the drinking and a pain pill that Diesel slipped into one of my shots several hours back now, I actually feel pretty good.

But it's fake, this feeling.

The pain will be back before I know it. Physical pain I can deal with though, losing Savannah this morning would be something else altogether.

Outside, the sky's turning that particular shade of Montana gray that comes right before the sun breaks the horizon. The air smells like dew, and dust, and the leftover exhaust from all the bikes that roared in through the night.

I light a cigarette, inhale deep enough to make my ribs scream, and look at the line of motorcycles against the garage wall. Every patch has been called in. Every fucking one.

Forty-seven bikes. Forty-seven votes.

Men stand in clusters near the church hall, smoking and talking low. They go quiet when they spot me. A few nod. Most just stare, faces blank as prison walls.

They know the rules. No lobbying. No pressure. No buying votes with promises or threats. The church vote is sacred—one of the few things we treat that way.

Doesn't stop the weight of their judgment from pressin' down on my shoulders like hands trying to force me to my knees.

I finish my smoke and flick the butt into the gravel. Time to face it.

The church hall door creaks when I push it open, like it's warning me to turn back. Inside, Brick, Ledger, Chains, Diesel, Ratchet, Roach, Havoc, and Butch are already moving around, setting up chairs in rows, pulling the long table to the front of the room.

Diesel spots me and breaks off, crossing the concrete

floor with his heavy steps that always sound like someone's about to get their skull caved in.

"There he is," he says, slapping me on the back hard enough to make me hiss from the screaming comin' off my ribs. "Ready for your big moment, brother?"

I nod, not trusting my voice yet. I've never asked for anything from the club. Never stood up and made my case for shit. I took my beatings, did my time, kept my mouth shut, and earned my patch with blood and silence.

Today I'll use my voice.

For her.

There are only three people on this earth I love— Mercy, Destiny, and Savannah. As my sisters, and as long as they are under twenty-one, Mercy and Destiny are automatically protected by the Club now that I'm patched in. Whether they want it or not.

But girlfriends are a whole other matter.

You gotta earn that protection. Because girlfriends, sex partners, even wives—they're very, very different than little sisters. They're risky. A hole in what otherwise might be tightly woven armor.

Did Savannah do enough last night to convince them? Was her submission satisfactory?

That's all that performance was. Submission. Will she follow my orders? Will she do what I tell her to, just because I tell her to?

"You know what you're gonna say?" Diesel asks, lowering his voice so the others can't hear. His eyes are serious under that permanent scowl.

"Yeah," I say, though I don't. Not really. I just know I'll say whatever I have to.

"Make it good," he says, and there's something in his tone that sounds like a warning. "Lots of brothers pretty upset about an Ashby under our roof."

"She's not an Ashby anymore," I say. "She's mine."

Diesel's face splits into a grin. "Yeah, we all saw that last night." He shakes his head. "Girl's got some fire in her, I'll give you that. But this ain't about how good she fucks, Legion. This is about the club."

"I know what it's about."

"Do you?" He steps closer, voice dropping to a whisper. "Because if this vote goes your way, you better be ready for what comes after. The Ashbys, the senator, the cops—they're all gonna come. And they're gonna come hard."

"I hope they do," I say. Meetin' his eyes. "They fucked up, Diesel. They fucked up. I will never get the image of Savannah tied to a bed, drugged and almost naked, out of my head. Not even killin' those boys would erase it. So let them come. I'll handle it."

Diesel studies me for a long moment, then nods once. "That's what I needed to hear." He claps me on the shoulder again. "You bleed for us. We bleed for you. That's the code."

The door opens, and men start filing in. Patches I recognize, some I don't. Older members I've only heard about in stories. Faces hard as stone, scarred from fights, weathered by years on the road.

Diesel gives me one last look before moving back to the table. "It's your show now, brother."

I stand to the side as they take their seats, row by row. The air in the room grows thick with tension and the smell of leather and sweat. This is church—our version of it, anyway. Where decisions are made that change lives.

End them, sometimes.

Brick calls the meeting to order with three strikes of the gavel. The sound echoes off the concrete walls like gunshots.

"Brothers," he says, his voice carrying to every corner of the room. "We're here for a Level-One vote. Patch member Legion Kane has called for club protection of a civilian—Savannah Ashby."

Murmurs ripple through the crowd. Some faces darken. Others remain impassive.

"As is our way," Brick continues, "he will present his case, and then we vote. No discussion. No debate. Just your conscience and the good of the club." He turns to me. "Brother Legion, the floor is yours."

I step up to the podium, feeling the weight of every set of eyeballs. My mouth is dry. My ribs ache with each breath. But none of that matters now.

What matters is Savannah, sleeping in my bed, with my mark on her chest and my name on her lips.

I look out at the sea of faces. Some nod encouragingly. Others glare, arms crossed over their chests, judgment already written in the hard lines around their mouths.

I take a breath and begin to speak for the only thing I've ever wanted to keep.

CHAPTER 11
SAVANNAH

I'm falling through darkness, tied to something I can't see. Cherry pie and Marcus's voice—*honey-dove, honey-dove*—his fingers on my face, in my hair, places I don't want him. The syringe coming closer, closer—

BANG!
BANG!
BANG!

I jolt upright, a scream lodged in my throat. My heart slams against my ribs as I blink at unfamiliar surroundings—cracked window repaired with duct tape, upside down milk crate, sheets that smell like Legion.

Legion. The silo. The rescue. The club.

I look down at my naked body tangled in rough sheets, chest still marked with Sharpie. *PROPERTY OF DEMON.* My wrists throb where the zip ties cut into them for three days.

BANG!
BANG!

BANG!

"Not Mine! Wake your ass up!"

Not Mine. I huff out a breath that's almost a laugh. It was cute last night when they christened me with whiskey and that ridiculous name, but in the cold light of morning, it feels less charming.

"I hear you breathing in there! When I fucking knock, Not Mine will get her ass up and answer the fucking door!"

The woman's voice is sharp as a cattle prod. Shit. I wrap the sheet around me, toga-style, and pull open the door with my heart still racing. I arrange my features into the polite mask I've worn at a thousand charity functions.

"How can I help you?" My voice comes out scratchy from sleep.

The silver-haired woman from last night stands in the doorway, arms crossed over her chest. She's wearing jeans and a faded Badlands MC tank top, her arms lean and muscled. Up close, I can see the lines around her eyes, the hardness in her jaw. This isn't a woman who's ever smiled for a camera she didn't want to.

"You've got thirty seconds to pull on some clothes," she barks, "otherwise you're coming with me naked."

I blink at her, still foggy from whatever drugs are lingering in my system.

"While the men do their little vote, us women have a meeting of our own," she explains. Though it is very clear that she doesn't feel explaining is necessary.

Great. A female interrogation to match the male one. Because showing my tits and fucking Legion in front of fifty bikers wasn't enough of an initiation.

But I nod anyway, because what choice do I have? I drop the sheet—the time for pretenses and privacy clearly over now—and pull yesterday's clothes back on. Legion's T-shirt hangs to my thighs, and clearly this little foray into kidnap-victim territory has caused me to lose weight, because the jeans have no intention of clinging to my hips this morning. I hold them up with one hand, nose crinkling because I now smell like spilled whiskey and stale ashes.

I sigh, wishing for more sleep. My body aches in places I don't want to think about, and I'm so hungry for more than liquid courage, my stomach is cramping.

But I follow the woman downstairs, feeling like I'm walking into judgment, as she leads me through a narrow hallway.

My bare feet stick slightly to the floor with each step.

God, I wish I had shoes.

"Where's Legion?" I ask.

She doesn't even turn around. "Church."

"Church." I sigh.

"The vote." She throws the words over her shoulder like I should know better than to ask. "When men decide things, they call it 'church'. When women decide things, they call it 'gossip'."

All right, then. She's friendly.

We reach a door at the end of the hallway, and she pushes it open without ceremony. The smell hits me first—burnt coffee and something fried hours ago. My stomach growls embarrassingly loud.

"Here," she says, gesturing me inside. "Sit."

The dining room isn't much of one. Just a scarred

wooden table surrounded by mismatched chairs that look like they were rescued from various yard sales and dumpsters. Faded wallpaper peels at the corners, showing layers beneath like geological strata. Grease marks map the wall near an ancient stove visible through a pass-through window.

A metal percolator hisses in the corner, spitting coffee that smells like it could strip paint. The morning light filters weakly through a single window crusted with dust, casting everything in a tired glow.

I sit where she points, at the head of the table. Not out of respect, I realize, but so everyone can see me. Observe me.

"I'm Mama Jo," she finally says, pouring herself coffee in a mug that reads WORLD'S OKAYEST MOM. "Diesel's old lady."

I nod, recognizing the name of the burly man who fed me shots last night. "I'm—"

"I know who you are," she cuts me off. "*Everyone* knows who you are."

She doesn't offer me coffee. I don't ask.

"OK." I shrink a little as the silence stretches between us, uncomfortable and deliberate. I resist the urge to fill it with pleasantries or questions. This isn't a Junior League tea. This is something else entirely.

Footsteps approach, and a woman appears in the doorway. She's maybe forty, with a practical bob and the upright posture of someone with a military background. She nods at Mama Jo, then looks at me with undisguised curiosity.

"June," Mama Jo says by way of introduction. "Havoc's wife."

June doesn't smile or extend her hand. Instead, she walks to the coffee pot, pours herself a cup, and then—oddly—places a folded white handkerchief on the table in front of me. It's pristine, with a delicate "J" embroidered in the corner.

I stare at it, confused, then look up to thank her or ask why, but she's already turning away, coffee in hand.

"Wait, what—" I begin, but Mama Jo shakes her head once, sharply.

I fall silent, fingering the handkerchief. It's real cotton, soft from many washings.

Before I can process this strange interaction, another woman enters. She's younger, covered in tattoos with a pierced septum and hair dyed an electric blue. She barely glances at me as she grabs coffee, but on her way out, she drops something that clinks against the table.

A brass coin. Heavy, and worn. Like it's been through a million hands. I squint to make out the lettering. *One Top-Shelf Drink*. What the... then I realize what this is. A bar token.

How odd. Why did she give it to me? I look up at Mama Jo, ready to ask questions, but she cuts me off with a cold expression. "That's Sienna," Mama Jo says after she's gone. "Roach's girl."

More women arrive, one after another. Some get coffee. Some just pass through. Each leaves something behind.

A tarnished bullet on a silver chain, dropped by a woman with a sleeve of watercolor tattoos. "It never fired when it should've," she mutters, the only one to speak directly to me. Mama Jo identifies her as Lita, Chain's partner.

A heavy, old-fashioned key, laid down deliberately by Mama Jo herself. "To nothing," she says when she catches me examining it. "Not anymore."

The pile grows. A woman whose name I never catch leaves behind a faded paperback with dog-eared pages. Another drops a small jar of what looks like homemade salve.

I sit still through it all, accepting each item without comment, though confusion and curiosity burn through me. This feels like a ritual, but no one bothers to explain the tradition.

The door bangs open harder than before, and a young woman with too much makeup and a crop top struts in like she owns the place. She looks barely twenty-one, with bleached hair and an expression that suggests she's perpetually smelling something unpleasant.

"Brandy," Mama Jo says, her tone noticeably cooler.

Brandy smirks at me, then dramatically drops a pair of motorcycle boots on the floor beside my chair. They land with a heavy thud.

"Those should fit," she sneers. "Though they might be a little *wide* for those skinny princess feet."

I blink at her hostility, so naked compared to the cool assessment of the others.

"Thank you," I say automatically, my mother's training kicking in.

Brandy snorts. "First one's free. And I'm not like the rest of them." She shoots Mama Jo a look. "If I came in with no shoes, that's what I'd want someone to give me. Not some stupid drink token or used-up handkerchief."

She flounces out without coffee, apparently just there for the delivery.

"Don't mind her," Mama Jo says after she's gone. "She's no one."

But Brandy was apparently listening around the corner, because she pops her head back in and snarls, "You wish, bitch." Then disappears again.

I'm aghast. And I clearly look it, because Mama Jo smiles at me, simply shrugging. "She hates me. But I hate her too. So it's even. One day, probably soon," Mama Jo says, calm as can be, "Brick will get tired of her skinny ass and that will be that. I will have my say and she will get the fuck out."

"Ohhhh Kaaay," I reply. Not sure what to think about that, but I am very appreciative for the boots.

More women file in—a steady stream of them. Many look like they've had hard lives—lined faces, tattoos that weren't done in proper shops, clothes that have seen better decades. Hangarounds, I'm told they're called. Women who aren't claimed by any one member.

Each one drops something. A faded t-shirt. Some pink shorts. A pair of jeans with a rip at the knee. A little dress with blue flowers on it. A tank top with the Badlands logo. Socks. A belt. A brush. Lip gloss.

By the time they're done, I have a small pile of clothing and accessories in front of me. None of it new. All of it worn. But enough to make at least three complete outfits.

I touch a denim jacket, fingers tracing a Badlands patch sewn over the heart. These women—who clearly have so little—just gave me their clothes.

"I don't understand," I finally say when the procession seems to have ended. "What is all this for?"

Mama Jo sips her coffee, regarding me over the rim. "What do you think it's for?"

I look at the pile. "For me to wear?"

"Smart girl," she says, not unkindly. "Since you came with nothing but what you had on."

I swallow hard. It's true. I have nothing. No phone, no wallet, no change of clothes. I'm literally wearing the shirt off Legion's back.

"But why would they—"

"Because I told them to," Mama Jo interrupts. "And they do what I say."

I nod slowly, fingering the soft denim of the jacket. "Should I... thank them?"

"No." Mama Jo stands and refills her coffee. "This isn't about gratitude."

"Then what is it about?"

She turns to face me, leaning against the counter. "It's about rules, Not Mine."

I wince at the nickname. "What rules?"

Mama Jo sets down her mug and approaches the table. She picks up the handkerchief, runs it through her fingers. "The first gift is free. Always. It's our way of saying maybe. Not yes. Just maybe." She places it back on the pile. "You take it, you owe nothin'."

I frown, not understanding.

"Any gift after the first," she continues, "is a contract. Silent. Unwritten. But real as hell. You take it, you owe somethin'." Her eyes bore into mine. "What you owe is never stated—but it will be decided by the person you owe. Could be loyalty. Could be protection. Could be silence. But you won't get to say no when it comes due."

The weight of her words settles over me. I look at the pile of offerings with new understanding.

"Don't worry about these," Mama Jo gestures to the pile. "Like I said, these ones are free. They don't cost nothin'. Not today. You take what's offered. You nod. That's all. But hear me good, girl—if they hand you somethin' tomorrow? You best know what that's worth before you reach."

I swallow hard, suddenly seeing these women in a whole new light. I don't know much about motorcycle clubs. I mean, basically, I know zero about motorcycle clubs. But it's very clear that the women don't have a say in what happens here.

At least... as far as the men are concerned.

But the biker culture isn't the only thing spinning inside this clubhouse.

There's a woman's culture too. Wife, or girlfriend, of the bikers.

And I'm part of that now.

"Do you understand what I'm telling you?" Mama Jo asks.

I nod slowly. "I think so."

"Good." She stands straighter. "Now put on those boots. No one in this club walks around barefoot. Makes us look like we can't provide."

I reach down and pick up the boots Brandy left. They're well-worn but solid. Black leather with silver buckles on the sides. I slip them on, and to my surprise, they fit perfectly.

"Thank you," I say quietly, not sure if I'm thanking Mama Jo, or Brandy, or all of them.

Mama Jo just nods. "The vote's done," she says, glancing at a clock I hadn't noticed. "They'll be out soon."

My heart skips. The vote. Legion. Whether I can stay or have to leave without him.

"You're in," she says.

"How do you know?" I ask.

Something that might be a smile touches Mama Jo's lips. "Because if it went the other way, Savannah Ashby, I wouldn't be wasting my time with you."

Relief floods through me so suddenly I feel dizzy. I'm staying. I'm in.

This place is... home.

"Now," Mama Jo says, picking up the denim jacket and holding it out to me. "Put this on. When they come in, you should look like you belong."

I take the jacket, feeling its weight, the history woven into its fibers. I slip it on over Legion's t-shirt. It fits like it was made for me.

Mama Jo looks me up and down, then nods once, satisfied.

"Almost there," she says. "Almost."

CHAPTER 12
LEGION

My name has always been plural.

Legion.

For we are many.

My mother named me after demons cast into swine. After spirits that spoke as one voice. Tonight, the many have spoken for me. A democracy of demons choosing mercy when they could have chosen exile.

The brand on my chest pulses with my heartbeat. Still infected. Still raw. Blood brotherhood isn't supposed to be clean.

The hall's quiet follows me like a ghost as I exit, lighting up a smoke. I pause, inhale, blow it out.

Forty-seven patched brothers.

Thirty-nine said yes.

Eight said no.

The numbers in my head feel like bullets left in a magazine after a firefight. Each one measured. Each one a threat or a promise.

Diesel walks beside me, quiet, like me. That's why I

like him. That's why he's my number one, no matter what.

I'm a thinker and he's a thinker too.

Problem is… there's a thing called over-thinking. And that's what I'm doing now.

Eight.

Eight.

Eight men said no.

I push open the door to the bar and the light hits me like judgment. Not the burning kind. The kind that shows you exactly what you are, scars and all.

Do the objections of eight men really matter when thirty-nine agreed?

Yes. Yes, they do.

Savannah will stay. She will be protected, even by those eight.

But there's always a cost. Always a debt.

I've never owned anything worth having that didn't eventually get taken away.

Not this time.

When I walk into the bar, everything stops. Not because of me—I'm just a vessel now, a conduit for what comes next.

She stands in the center of the room, transformed.

Savannah. But not Savannah. Not the Ashby princess I've known since she was twelve. Not the Instagram queen with the practiced smile. Something else entirely.

The denim jacket hangs off her shoulders, a single patch above her heart with the Badlands logo. Her feet, bare last night while she stood trembling, now anchored in biker boots. Her hair's pulled back, messy but deliberate.

The Sharpie marks on her chest peek out where the t-shirt cuts low. PROPERTY OF DEMON.

My claim in black ink.

God I love her. She's worth everything to me. And even though I couldn't say it last night or it would've turned out different this morning, if she left, I would've left with her.

I would've taken my chances.

Maybe they really would kill me. It's happened before. I haven't seen it, obviously. It took me thirteen fucking years to earn my patch for reasons I won't get in to. And that means I never really belonged. There were always secrets between me and my Badlands brothers. Prospects get left out of business like that.

But I would've risked it. I would've hoped that I had the respect from enough of them that I'd be the one to walk away clean.

I love these men like brothers. Brick, maybe even like a father.

But there will never be another Savannah Ashby in my life.

Mine.

Today, though—I don't have to think about that.

Only eight, I remind myself.

Only eight.

Savannah is neither Ashby nor outsider now. She's something undefined. Something dangerous, for sure.

My eyes trace the edges of her silhouette, seeing in her the same war that's etched across my skin—the angel and the demon locked in eternal combat.

"You good?" I ask, walking towards her with my hand out, ready to touch what's mine.

She nods once. Doesn't smile.

Smiles are for cameras and liars.

I feel the brand on my chest throb in time with my pulse. The angel's sword piercing the demon's heart—the war I carry everywhere.

The ink that tells my story so I don't have to speak it.

And then, the mood changes. A celebration swells around us like high tide. Music is softer now. Not the rage of last night's claim.

The welcoming of a new woman is a softer affair.

I lead her to the center of the room. Savannah and I start pressed together, her hip against mine, my hand on the small of her back. We dance. We linger together. A team. We keep hold of each other as the hours pass.

But as the day deepens, as the evening draws near, we drift.

Not apart—just finding our orbits.

I lean against the wall, nursing a beer I've barely touched. My ribs throb with each breath, but pain's just background noise now. Always has been.

Savannah moves through the crowd like she was born to it. My brothers part for her, some with respect, some with hunger they know better than to act on. Her golden hair catches the dim light, a halo against the smoke and darkness. Strange how something so bright can belong in a place built from shadows.

I don't need to guard her every step anymore. She's claimed now. Protected. But my eyes follow her anyway, tracking her path through the bodies and bottles. It's instinct, like my fingers finding the outline of angels on my skin during those sleepless nights in The Pit.

"Your girl's a natural," Diesel says, appearing beside me. "Didn't expect that."

I nod, watching Savannah laugh at something Chains says. "She's adaptable."

"Eight votes against," Diesel mutters. "That's eight brothers waitin' for you to slip."

In prison, I read the Bible cover to cover three times. Not from faith—from boredom and the need for stories bigger than concrete walls. Mark 5:9 gave me my name, but it's what came after that haunts me now. The demons begged not to be sent away. They pleaded to remain among the living, among the familiar.

I understand their fear now. The terror of exile from what you love.

The Ashbys won't let this stand. I know that. They don't surrender daughters to men like me.

Across the room, Savannah catches my eye. Holds it. Something passes between us—not a smile, something deeper. A recognition. A choice being made again, in real time.

I wonder if Savannah and I are writing the same tale now—outcasts by choice, marked by what we've chosen to love despite the cost.

I stand in the corner watching my brothers celebrate what they don't understand. They think this is about pussy or power—something simple. Something they can name. But what's between Savannah and me isn't just blood, or bone, or breath.

It's older than that. Deeper.

The beer bottle sweats against my palm, cold glass

against hot skin. I take small sips, letting the bitter taste linger like the memories of The Pit.

It's just solitary.

But it's so much more than solitary.

The Pit is a darkness, an emptiness, a sense of being hallowed out.

But I never did mind that feeling.

I like the darkness.

We are Legion. We are many.

"So...." Ledger appears at my elbow.

"So," I offer back.

"It wasn't personal."

I look Ledger in the eyes. Shrug a shoulder. "I know that. You don't have to explain."

"I only voted no because... well." He blows out a breath. "It just doesn't add up, Legion. It doesn't. And it never will. I hope I'm wrong, I really do. But I don't think I am. So I voted no."

I take another pull from my bottle. "I understand."

He claps me on the back. "She's real pretty though. Not gonna hear me complain about having to see her face for the rest of my days." Then he walks off before I can respond.

I've spent most of my life being the demon they named me. The monster under Drybone's collective bed. But monsters serve a purpose too. They keep the real predators at bay.

My eyes drift across the room, pulled by the high whine of a tattoo machine. The sound cuts through the music and laughter like a blade through skin.

Savannah sits in Chains' chair, wrist held in his hand. Her face is calm, almost serene, as the needle pierces her skin again and again. I walk over, wondering what the hell is going on.

But I'm truly, truly speechless when I look down and see what she's getting.

PROPERTY OF DEMON is spelled out letter by letter in stark black, just above the raw circle of newly-scabbed skin from the restraints that held her prisoner just 24 hours ago.

Demon.

I'd rather wish it said Legion, but I guess they are one and the same.

Chains finishes with a flourish, wiping excess ink from Savannah's wrist.

Pride fills my chest, a heat that burns hotter than the infected brand beneath my shirt. This claiming goes both ways now.

My mark on her, her choice made permanent.

"There," Chains says, applying ointment and clear wrap. "Keep it covered for two hours, then wash with unscented soap."

The tattoo sits on her inner wrist where her pulse beats strongest. Where life flows. Where veins run closest to the surface.

I think of the massive piece sprawlin' across my back—the war between realms, the fallen angels hunting demons, the judgment and fire. The final panel on my lower back shows an angel with burned wings standing before a sealed gateway. Behind him, smoke rises. Ahead, emptiness.

My body tells a story of violence and vengeance, of holy war and fallen grace.

And now Savannah carries a chapter of that same

story on her skin. Not as victim. Not as trophy. But as willing participant in our shared mythology.

The music changes, somethin' low and heavy with bass that vibrates through the floorboards. Savannah looks up at me, eyes clear despite the whiskey and whatever drugs still linger in her system. "Dance with me," she says.

I take her hand, careful of the fresh ink, and lead her to the small space where couples sway in the half-dark. I pull her against me, one hand on the small of her back, the other tangled in her hair.

Our bodies move together like we've practiced this a thousand times. Maybe we have, in dreams or past lives or the spaces between heartbeats.

We wrap this party up the same way we started it.

There's something holy in symmetry like that.

My ribs protest with each breath. My face throbs where Cash's fists connected. But these pains feel almost holy now—stigmata earned in service of something greater than myself.

On my spine, a blindfolded angel holds a demon by the throat in eternal judgment. Barbed vines twist through the demon's ribs, pulled from the ground below. The angel has no weapon—only judgment.

Yet here, in this moment, there is no judgment—only acceptance as complete as the ink that covers me from neck to waist.

Savannah presses her forehead against my chest, right over the infected brand. "I love you," she whispers, so soft only I can hear.

"Mine," I say into her hair.

I hold her closer, our hips moving in slow circles as

the bass thumps like a heartbeat around us. I wonder if this is what peace feels like—not the absence of war, but the absolute certainty of which side you're fighting for.

The alarm rips through the clubhouse like a knife, shrill and demandin'.

The transformation is instant—almost beautiful in its precision.

Music cuts off mid-beat.

Laughter dies in throats.

Weapons materialize from hidden holsters and beneath tables.

I watch my brothers shift from celebration to defense. The way they move reminds me of the war inked across my back—my personal apocalypse rendered in black and gray. The descent of armored angels, wings unfurled, weapons drawn. Divine wrath made flesh.

My body responds before my mind catches up, muscle memory taking over. The lover recedes, the fighter emerges. This change isn't new. It's as familiar as breathing, as inevitable as the flames that lick up my ribcage in layered grayscale, consuming everything soft.

"Three at the gate," Roach calls out, hunched over a security monitor. "Luxury ride. Ashby logo on the car."

Diesel appears at my side, shotgun in hand. "You expecting company?"

He knows I'm not. But something cold slides down my spine as I move toward the monitor. The camera feed shows a black Range Rover idling at our gate. Two figures visible through the windshield.

"Fuck me," I mutter, leaning closer. "It's Colt."

But it's not *just* Colt.

The passenger seat holds someone I haven't seen in three years.

"Destiny," I say. "My sister."

But there's somethin'—some*one*—small in her arms.

The baby.

"Open it," I say, straightening.

Roach looks to Brick, who gives a tight nod. "Let 'em through. But only to the lot."

I feel every eye in the room burning into my back as I walk toward the door. The weight of their doubt presses down on my shoulders like the crown of thorns worn by the lead angel in my tattoo—the one diving from heaven with a flaming spear.

I don't need to hear the whispers to know what they're thinking.

Eight men.

Eight nos.

Eight who think I've lost my edge, compromised the club, invited war to our doorstep.

And now, seeing Colt Ashby bringing my post-pregnant runaway sister back, those eight are probably eighteen.

Savannah moves to follow me, but I stop her with a look. "Stay inside."

"Legion—"

"Just... *wait*." My voice comes out harder than I meant it to.

Outside, the night air hits my face like a slap. The lot is bathed in harsh floodlights, turnin' everything stark white or pitch black. No shadows, no gray areas. Just like the club sees the world.

The Range Rover rolls to a stop twenty feet away. The driver's door opens, and Colt steps out, hands visible. Smart move.

"Legion," he calls. "We need to talk."

I walk forward slowly, aware of at least five guns trained on Colt from various windows. My own piece sits heavy against my lower back, tucked into my jeans.

"About what?" I ask, stopping ten feet away.

"About her." Colt nods toward the passenger side.

The door opens, and Destiny slides out. She looks thinner than I remember, her face sharper. But her eyes are the same—our mother's eyes, defiant even when afraid. In her arms, wrapped in a pale-yellow blanket, is a tiny sleepin' face.

My niece or nephew. Blood of my blood.

And there it is.

The truth.

The eight dissenters saw what I refused to see.

This was never just about Savannah and me.

This was about worlds colliding—Ashby wealth against Kane poverty, political power against outlaw justice, inheritance against survival.

"Legion," Destiny says, her voice smaller than I remember. "I'm sorry. It's just... I wanted you to see her and I couldn't wait no more."

She slides an eye over to Colt.

And suddenly it all makes sense.

Why he helped me.

So I would not kill him when this moment came.

I take another step forward, close enough now to see the dark circles under my sister's eyes, the way her hands tremble slightly as she holds her child.

Battle lines aren't drawn in sand. But in blood, and ink, and history.

My name echoes in my head—Legion, for we are many—and I understand now that the war tattooed across my body was never just decoration.

It was prophecy.

I pull my gun out of my pants and aim it at Colt Ashby's head.

END OF BOOK SHIT

Welcome to the End of Book shit. This is the part of the book where I get to say anything I want about the book you just read. Thoughts about what was on my mind, my plans, how it turned out, why I wrote it—stuff like that.

I'm going to preface this with a note about EOBS in books 3 and 4. I'm not going to write them. The EOBS in book 1 was from last year (2025) because I was making an omnibus version of the paperback for my 12 Days of Giveaways in December. That's it. The only reason it was written. So it's a little outdated but also contains good thoughts about the series when it was written. Thoughts I don't particularly remember now, because I wrote these novellas in spring of 2025, which is nearly a year ago now.

So this EOBS is more current. And because these are

novellas, how much can one author really say about 35,000 words?

The next EOBS will be in book 5.

Then we can talk about all the things… :)

Also, the FBI Book Club was a fun little bonus in book 1, but they read ahead mo-fo's! There's nothing to talk about until book 5, then we'll see if Kowalski is still breathing or her if DNR order was absolute… I have a feeling she might be *dramatic* about that ending…

So. Let's talk about what you just watched happen.

Savannah Ashby — ranch princess, four million followers, seventy thousand photographs of a perfectly curated life — just stripped naked on a couch in front of forty-seven patched bikers and let a man write PROPERTY OF DEMON across her chest in Sharpie.

And then she turned around and screamed it at the room like a war cry.

And you didn't stop reading.

You might be sitting with that right now. Might be asking yourself some uncomfortable questions. Like why that scene didn't make you angry. Why it made you feel something closer to relief. Why watching a woman who spent her entire life being owned by cameras and obligations and a dead mother's ghost and a senator's son who tied her to a bed and drugged her for three days — why watching that woman CHOOSE to bare her body on her own terms felt less like degradation and more like the first free breath she's taken in thirty years.

Because that's the thing about the claiming that I need you to understand.

Marcus took. He restrained her. Sedated her. "Cleaned" her. Called it love. Called it rescue. Performed ownership over her unconscious body and called it protection.

Legion asked.

And she said yes.

With her eyes open. With a room full of dangerous men watching. With the full weight of what it meant sitting on her chest. She said yes. And then she got his name tattooed on her wrist — right over the scabs where the zip ties cut into her skin.

That's not submission.

That's a woman burning her own house down and choosing exactly where to stand in the fire.

Now let me tell you why I wrote it like that. Because I know some of you are wondering.

I grew up on the edges of MC culture in northeastern Ohio. Early 80s. Lake Erie cold. Rust-belt broke. The kind of place where boys turned into one of two things by eighteen — strangers, because they left. Or bikers, because they stayed.

This was before Metallica made metal cool. Before Sons of Anarchy made the cut romantic. This was boots, and flannels, and chips on shoulders the size of the recession. I was a kid seeing things my brain wasn't old enough to file correctly.

Men who would die for each other on Monday and beat each other bloody by Friday. Women who stayed.

Not because it was romantic. Because they had kids, and nowhere else to go, and love looks different when you're poor.

But here's what nobody talks about — the women who stayed and MEANT it. Not the ones who were trapped. The ones who chose. The ones who looked at the violence, and the brotherhood, and the leather, and the brand and said *this is mine and I will kill to keep it.*

That's not a love story the way most people write it.

That's a blood oath.

And Savannah just signed hers.

On a couch. In front of witnesses. With Sharpie on her skin and then ink in her skin and her whole life burning behind her like a mansion she'll never go back to.

So if you came into this series thinking Legion was the dangerous one —

Adjust.

Because that woman just let a leaked video of her go viral, tattooed an outlaw's name over her wounds, and told a room full of criminals she belongs to the most dangerous man in Montana.

And she smiled when she said it.

Not the smile her mother taught her. Not the one she performs for cameras.

A real one.

The first real one.

If you've got a problem with the act itself, I.e. - well, this isn't the kind of book meant to be read in public. But it IS the kind of book where a woman gives her man a blow job in front of a clubhouse of bikers because she knows everything comes with a cost.

If you needed a content warning about that scene, then here it is: She liked it.

If you need permission to like it too — you don't. You already do. That's why you're still here.

This isn't a romance that saves you. This isn't a romance that holds your hand. This is a baptism in blood and if you're not ready to get messy, this isn't your series.

The door is not open. The door is OFF. The hinges are in a ditch somewhere.

Legion fell first. Fell hardest. Has been falling since he was fourteen years old.

But Savannah just jumped.

And she is not looking for a net.

Book Three drops in seven days. Bring a glass of water and lower your expectations for productivity.

I'm not even a little sorry. I will do it again.

Thank you for reading, thank you for reviewing, and I'll see you in the next book…

Julie

JA Huss

February 7, 2026

Book of Legion - Badlands MC #3

SCARS
& promises

New York Times Bestselling Author
JA HUSS

How far will you go for the club.
How much will you give for the patch.
It better be everything, or there will be consequences.

Property of.
Infected brand.
Angels and demons.

The backside of twenty-three?

SCARS AND PROMISES

The cruelest thing hope ever did was show up.

ABOUT THE AUTHOR

JA Huss is a scientist, New York Times and USA Today bestselling author. Her self-published romantasy Sparktopia was named an Audible Editors' Best of the Year selection in 2024, and several of her audiobooks have been nominated for the Audie and SOVA Awards. A 2019 RITA finalist, Huss has also had five books optioned for film and television.

(My real bio, since the last one was a front... lol)

www.ingramcontent.com/pod-product-compliance
Lightning Source LLC
LaVergne TN
LVHW090041080526
838202LV00046B/3911